BURN THE DEAD

PURGE

STEVEN JENKINS

BURN THE DEAD: PURGE

BOOK TWO

Copyright © 2015 by Steven Jenkins

Published in Great Britain in 2015 by Different Cloud Publishing.

www.steven-jenkins.com

Contents

"For Dad."

FREE BOOK

"If you love scary campfire stories of ghosts, demonology, and all things that go bump in the night, then you'll love this horror collection by author Steven Jenkins."

COLIN DAVIES – Director of BAFTA winning BBC's The Coalhouse.

For a limited time only, you can download a **FREE** copy of Spine - the latest horror collection from Steven Jenkins.

FIND OUT MORE HERE

www.steven-jenkins.com

PROLOGUE

Can't sleep again. Too cold.

Dad won't switch on the central heating, says it's too expensive. He tells me to use the spare blanket. But I hate using that. It's so itchy, and there're spiders in the cupboard. Dad tries to teach me to face my fears, says I'm a silly little girl for being afraid of a furry bug. But he just doesn't get it. I'm thirteen years old, and I'll be fourteen in a month—so if I haven't got over my arachnophobia by now, then I guess I'm stuck with it. For life.

I switch the TV on. Sometimes watching some shitty film manages to knock me out, but the volume has to be low. Can't disturb Mum and Dad—Dad will kill me. He's already threatened to take the TV away if I wake him again. He tells me that I'll understand when I finally go out into the real world, working, earning a living. The usual grown-up crap.

At least I wouldn't scrimp on the heating.

Another hour passes and I switch the TV off. There's nothing on apart from shopping channels and weird reality shows. Not my cup of tea. Mum loves that kind of rubbish, but I can't see the attraction. Most of the girls in my class watch them. But I guess I've always been a little different. I'd rather be watching action movies, or shows about police arresting drunks. The kind of junk Dad watches.

Almost four in the morning and I'm still wide-awake. Got school tomorrow. Can't see me being too alert for maths first thing. I'll have to sit in the back, try to avoid eye contact with Mr Morgan. I should be all right. He usually picks on the boys. Plus, he has a soft spot for me and Chrissie. He always smiles at us in the corridor. It's not as creepy as it sounds. He used to live next door to Uncle Pete. It's weird seeing teachers outside of school. Not sure why. It just is.

Need a pee. Not desperate but once the thought pops into my head, I'll never get to sleep. Best get it done now rather than lying here thinking about it for another two hours, so I get up and tiptoe onto the landing. Mum and Dad's bedroom door is half-open, so I move even slower, holding my breath as I get to the bathroom. Once inside, I lock it and sit on the toilet. So glad it finally has a lock on it. It took Dad ages to finally get one. He's always been against locks in the house. Don't know how many times I've asked him for one for my room. Can't see that happening any time soon. Maybe when I'm twenty-five and married, with kids of my own.

I finish up, flush and start to wash my hands. The sink is directly under the window, which looks onto the garden. Most people have frosted glass in the bathroom, but of course Dad has to be awkward. Just pathetic, flimsy blinds that get tangled if you pull too hard. Dad says that there's a knack to it, that I'm doing it wrong. Most of the time I just roll my eyes, (after he's gone, obviously). Drying my hands with the towel, I look down at the pitch-black garden. Can't see a thing apart from the thick oak trees and the outline of the shed. But the more I stare, the more my eyes adjust, the more I'm certain that I see a person standing next to the tree.

Can't be.

I climb onto the bathtub and pull open the top window. Poking my head out into the cold air, I take a closer look. It still seems like a person, dressed in white, with a slim body, and not that tall; but it's too dark to be sure. Maybe I should call Dad? In case it's a burglar? No, he'd kill me; he'd tell me it's just the trees and my lack of sleep playing tricks on me.

But what if he's wrong? What if it is a burglar? And I *didn't* say something?

Best be certain before I wake him. If I can get the garden light sensor to come on, then I'll be sure. Bending down, I pick up one of Mum's fancy soaps, the ones she never uses, then push my head and shoulders out into the cold night air. I see the figure again. It creeps me out. It's not moving so it might be some branches, or some rubbish that's blown into the garden. The light sensor is to the left of me, so I launch the soap near it, praying that I don't hit Mum and Dad's window by mistake. The soap hits the wall and then drops down onto the grass below, with virtually no noise at all. But the sensor doesn't catch it, and the garden is still in darkness.

Bloody hell!

Still leaning against the frame of the open window, I glare at the so-called figure. But the more

I look at it, and the more it sways slightly from side to side, the more certain I am that it *is* a person. Still not sure enough to wake Dad. Not yet, anyway. I need more evidence.

I leave the bathroom and tiptoe downstairs. The last few steps are really creaky so I avoid them, lunging my leg past them to reach the bottom. Creeping into the living room, I automatically flick the light switch, but then immediately turn it off. I'll see better into the garden without it. Over at the glass patio doors, I push a few blinds over to the side to see outside.

My heart judders as I stare into the pale face of a woman.

I let go of the blinds and dash out of the living room, heart racing, and scramble up the stairs to wake Dad. Opening the bedroom door, I poke my head through. They're both still fast asleep, so I reach down and prod Dad on his shoulder. "Dad," I whisper. "Wake up. There's a woman outside."

Dad begins to stir and then his eyes half-open. "Go back to bed," he mumbles. "It's just a nightmare, sweetheart."

11

He shuts his eyes, so I prod him again. "Dad. Wake *up*. There *is* someone outside. I think it's a burglar."

Dad opens his eyes again, sits up in bed, and switches his bedside lamp on. "What are you talking about?"

"There's a woman standing in our garden."

"Are you sure?"

"Yes, Dad. I'm positive. I saw her standing by the patio doors."

He climbs out of bed, puts his slippers on and follows me out onto the landing. "Stay here," he says firmly, and I watch him as he walks downstairs. From the landing, I can see him enter the living room. Can't help but feel nervous. Dad could easily defend himself against anyone, especially a woman. But you never know. She might have a knife. Or a gun!

I'd better go help him.

Moving fast but quietly down the stairs, my mind fills with visions of Dad being shot by the burglar. Can't think like that. Dad's strong and he's not an idiot. He'd never let it come to that.

Inside the dark living room, I see him pressed against the wall, with his head peering through the blinds. I creep over to him. "Can you see her?"

"Bloody hell!" Dad blurts out in fright as he turns to face me. "I told you to wait upstairs! Why don't you ever listen to me?"

"Sorry, Dad."

Shaking his head, he returns his attention to the window.

"Can you see her?" I repeat. "Is she still out there?"

"I can't see anyone. Are you sure you saw someone? It's pretty dark out there."

"Yes, Dad. I'm sure. She was standing by the tree, and when I came down to the living room she was by the glass, looking right at me. I swear it."

Moving away from the window, Dad walks past me and out through the doorway.

"Where are you going?"

He doesn't answer, so I follow. He walks down the hallway and into the dark kitchen.

"Stay back now," he orders. "I'm going outside to check. Maybe it's just some drunk from town, wandered into the garden."

"Shouldn't we just call the police?"

"Not yet. And keep that light off."

I nod as Dad opens the door. A sudden gust of cold air hits us both in the face. "Be careful," I say, my stomach full of butterflies. Then he steps outside and closes the door behind him.

Standing in the kitchen, in silence, for what seems like an eternity, I listen out for something, anything. I can feel my hands shaking as I stare at the door handle. *Please be okay, Dad.*

As the seconds turn into minutes, I find myself edging closer and closer to the back door. Curiosity has always been my weakness, (or strength, depending on how you look at it). Maybe I should just open the door and pop my head out, just to check if he's all right. Surely he won't get mad. I won't actually be following him—just having a nose.

Another minute or so passes and I've reached the handle, grasped it and started to turn it. Don't know how much help I can be if Dad's really in trouble, but I have to at least try. Chest tight, I slowly open the door, one inch at a time.

Suddenly, the outside light comes on and the back door bursts open.

I'm flung backwards onto the floor, hitting my head on the fridge.

I see Dad, rushing to get the door shut and locked, his face white, his eyes wide, like he's just seen a ghost. But before he can pull the bolt across to lock it, the door flies open, knocking him to the floor, his body landing on top of mine. The blonde woman is standing in the doorway, snarling like a dog; her eyes grey. The moment she spots us on the floor, she lunges towards us. Dad lifts both his legs up and manages to catch her body with the soles of his feet, and then pushes her back towards the opening. She lands hard onto her back, howling as she scrambles to her feet. Dad quickly gets up off the floor, his hands stretched out in front, ready for a second attack. I try to follow him, but I'm frozen. All I can do is cower further back against the fridge, behind his legs. The woman darts towards Dad again, black spit oozing from her mouth, her arms reaching forward. Dad secures both her wrists and wrestles her backwards towards the door. I watch in horror as the woman tries to pull Dad's arm towards her open mouth.

"Leave him alone!" I scream as I get up off the floor.

I see Dad's golf clubs, propped up in their bag against the table. Hauling out one of his putts, I hold it up like a shotgun, aim the metal end forwards, and then drive it into the woman's face, splitting her nose like a peach. The distraction is enough for Dad to push her outside into the garden. But she still has a firm hold of his wrists, pulling him out with her. Just as I'm about to take another stab with the putt, I hear a thud.

Suddenly the woman lets go of Dad's wrists and drops to her knees, eyes still wide open.

She collapses onto her back.

From the darkness of the garden, someone steps out. A man. He's wearing white padded overall, white gloves, black boots, and has a helmet over his head. In his hand is a strange gun, pointed down at the woman. Dad steps back into the kitchen, pulling me behind him.

"Who *is* that?" I ask Dad in disbelief, as the fear

started to fade—much faster than I thought it would.

"It's a *Cleaner.*"

"A Cleaner?"

"Not that type of a cleaner, sweetheart. A different one."

"What's wrong with that woman?"

Dad pushes me further back into the kitchen. "She's infected. She's not well."

I look up at Dad. "Is she a zombie?"

Dad nods, his eyes still gigantic.

"Get back!" the man orders as he straps something over the woman's mouth. "And lock that door! Now!"

That was amazing! Wait 'til Chrissie hears about this!

"I know what I want to be when I grow up," I say as Dad starts to close the back door.

"What's that, sweetheart?"

"I want to be a Cleaner."

Dad locks the door, and the dead woman disappears from view.

"A Cleaner?" Dad asks, as he rushes to the kitchen window.

17

"Yeah."

He pulls the blind over to one side, looks outside, and then turns to me. *"Not a bloody chance."*

1

Nerves start to slither over me as I reach the steel gates. I can't see any signs on the building, which looks to me like a small warehouse, or a factory. *Strange.* Pulling out the piece of paper from my jeans pocket, I double-check the address.

This is *the right place. Don't panic.*

I push the gate open; it creaks noisily as the bottom scrapes against the concrete.

Inside the car park I see a large white van and two cars. I walk over to what seems to be the entrance. As I reach for the door handle, I can't help but wonder if all this is just a cruel prank and there is no actual job. I mean, who the hell would want *me* as a Cleaner, anyway? It's not like I have any real experience in security. I should have lied on my CV. *Everyone does it.* I should have told them that I'd worked as a bouncer for a year or two. Made up some pub, maybe; one that's already closed down, in case they check up on me.

I push and pull the door handle but nothing happens. *Locked!* This *is* a wind-up. But how *can* it be? The Job Centre gave me the address. Must be a different place then; maybe it's on the other side of Ammanford. I see a security keypad on the wall. I push the button with the bell symbol on it, half expecting it not to work. I can just about hear a faint buzzing sound echoing inside.

I wait.

I've got the wrong place.

I've buggered up my *only* interview. *Nice one, Cath—you've blown your dream job before it's even begun.* How *dumb* can you get? After all the letters you sent, all the complaints you filed that women could just as easily do the job—and you go and mess up the bloody address.

Genius!

Walking away from the doors, I pull out my mobile phone from my handbag. Job Centre didn't give a contact number, but I should be able to find it online, though. I remove my woollen gloves, slip them into my coat pocket and push the *Internet* button. Just as it connects, I hear the door opening. There's a tall man standing in the doorway. He's in his late-fifties, completely bald and wearing a shirt and tie; his top button is undone.

"Catherine? Catherine Woods?" the man asks, his voice deep and husky, his eyes telling me that I am expected, but not welcome.

At least I'm in the right place.

He shakes my hand, squeezing it way too tight. Not sure if it's just a force of habit, or some macho thing. I expect he does that to most men he meets, just to showcase strength and authority. But what the hell would he get from doing it to a woman? I think it's already established from his size that he's stronger than me, that he could kick my ass in his sleep.

"Hi," I say, prying my hand from his grip, "you must be Mr Davies."

"Yeah, that's me. Did you find the place all right?"

"I found it fine, thanks. Just wasn't sure that I got the right address. Couldn't see any signs outside."

"I know, it's confusing. We try to keep the place low-key. The Job Centre should've mentioned it."

"It's okay. No big deal."

"Shall we get started then, Catherine?"

I smile politely, but I'm guessing he already hates my guts, thinks I'm not right for the job. But I'm here now, no turning back. All he can say is *No, thank you. Better luck next time.*

"So," I say, trying to break the silence as we walk along the grey corridors; my voice and footsteps echoing, "do many people know what this building is used for?"

"No, not many. Well, apart from the government, the staff, families, and probably a few others. I mean, it's not like Area 51 or anything. It's almost impossible to keep secrets these days. But it helps to stop the locals from freaking out. Last thing we want is complaints, or idiots snooping around at night. It's way too dangerous."

"Why's that? I didn't think you kept any inventory at your base. I thought they got sent for burning."

Mr Davies stops at a door, grasps the handle and then turns to me. "Not all the time."

I follow him inside. He takes my coat and scarf and directs me to a chair next to a wooden desk. I sit down, my body rigid with anxiety, as he walks around to the other side of the desk and sinks into a leather chair. Leaning back, he looks me straight in the eye; his stare untrusting, like a cop trying to get information out of a suspect. "So, Catherine," he says, putting both his hands behind his head, "we've got five hardworking Cleaners in our branch, so what's the fascination about becoming our sixth member? I mean, it's dangerous, underpaid, and quite frankly very unappealing for anyone—let alone a woman. There must be hundreds of jobs out there for a pretty young girl like you."

Nice.

"Well, Mr Davies—"

"Call me Roger, sweetie," he corrects me, his patronising tone causing my clammy fists to clench as they rest on my thighs.

I force a good-mannered smile. "Okay. Well...*Roger*, all my life I've wanted to be a Cleaner. Ever since I was a little girl, I've wanted to protect people. And what better way than to work in this field. I mean, there's nothing like it. It's the frontline. The most important part of the fight."

23

He nods along. I can tell he thinks I'm full of shit, that I'm just talking the talk. He picks up a sheet of paper from the desk, glances at it and then squints his eyes. "Says here that you're twenty-three years old. Is that correct?"

I nod. "Yes, that's right Mr—I mean, Roger. Twenty-three last month."

"Aren't you a little bit *young* to be out on the frontline? Risking your life?"

"Well, if I may, *Roger*, a lot of soldiers risking their lives on the frontline are younger than me. Some as young as eighteen."

"Yes, but you're not a soldier, Catherine." He squints again at the sheet of paper, which is clearly a copy of my CV. "Says here that you dropped out of the Territorial Army after just two years of service." He locks his eyes on mine again. "Why was that Catherine?"

"I injured my knee playing hockey," I say, rubbing my left knee. "Twisted it pretty badly. Had to have surgery. So I spent the next few years getting my strength back. But it's fine now. Good as new."

"So why didn't you just re-join? I'm sure they would have been more than happy to take you back."

"I wanted to, but I got a full-time job in the restaurant, which meant working most weekends, so there was just no way to commit to re-joining."

"Okay, that's understandable, Catherine, we all need to work. However, you may have to carry heavy equipment. Is that going to be a problem with a dodgy knee?"

"Absolutely not. As I said, it's as good as new. But I'll be fine with any heavy inventory. I've been training hard for the past few years; strength training, lots of uphill running, cycling."

"Some of the inventory might be *extremely* heavy. Are my guys going to be stuck carrying your workload?"

"No, Roger. I can carry my own inventory. I promise."

He groans, and then takes another look at my CV. "Says here that you're born and raised in Ammanford. Will it be a problem for you travelling all around South and West Wales? Some days we're not back until the early hours of the morning."

"Not at all. This is something that I've always wanted to do. I know it's a tough job, but that's one of the reasons why it's so important to me. I love a challenge. And I'm not scared of anything."

"Well you *should* be. This job is not what the papers say. They make out that it's all glamorous, that it's going in all guns blazing. But I can assure you, Catherine, that it's most definitely *not*. I've lost three good men over the past five years, and every one of those men had families, friends. But one tiny mistake, one unpredictable situation they couldn't control, and that's it. *Gone*," he clicks his fingers, "just like that."

"I promise you, applying for this job was not something I took lightly."

"Well, you did a little more than just *apply* for the job, Catherine. Thanks to your many letters of complaint to the government, which were handed directly to me, we've had to change our policy on employing women. Now I know it may *seem* sexist to you, and probably to all women out there. But Catherine, let me tell you that nothing is ever black and white. If our department feels that it's necessary that only *men* are employed, then that is for the safety of the public and my team. I don't give a shit if that comes across negative, or sexist, or *whatever*. My only concern is the lives around me. Do you understand?"

"Yes I do, Roger. And I completely trust that every decision you make is for the good of the team. But I'm a very proactive woman. I saw an opportunity to make a change, to follow a dream, to make a difference, and I took it."

"Either way you look at it, thanks to equality, I have no choice now but to open the doors to female applicants. And seeing as you were the *only* woman who's applied to this branch," he puts the CV down and gets up from his chair, reaching across the desk, "welcome aboard."

I smile and shake his hand. "Thank you, Roger. You won't regret it. I promise."

He sits back down, groans again, and then runs his hands over his smooth head. "I hope not, Catherine. For your sake, as well as mine."

2

"So when does the training start?" Dad asks me, slurping his tea from across the breakfast table.

"I already said, Dad," I reply, unable to disguise the impatience in my voice. "This weekend. Thursday is a run through—meet the guys, kind of an intro. Plus, a fitness test. If that goes well, the real training will start on Friday."

"For how long?"

"Until Sunday."

"Until *Sunday?*" he blurts out, almost spitting out his tea. "That's it?"

"Well, yeah. But it's very intense. And most of the important training is done out on the field. I'll be shadowing someone first. Then, maybe after a few weeks, maybe even a few months, I'll be having to deal with things alone."

"One bloody weekend. That's scandalous. You'd swear you were training to work in a supermarket—not working as a bloody Cleaner." He takes a giant—almost *aggressive* swig of his tea—and puts his cup down a little too hard on the table, spilling a little. "All I hear on the News is how little money they get from the government, putting up with shitty equipment, understaffing, and dangerous working conditions. It's just not worth the risk."

"Tell that to the armed forces then. They've always had to put up with budget cuts. And so has the NHS. But we still need nurses and soldiers."

"Well, I think you're mad, Catherine. I really do. And I don't see what the big fascination is with all this. Why can't you just get an ordinary job like everyone else?"

"I know it's risky, but this is something that I've wanted to do since I was a little girl. *You* know that. So nothing's changed. I still want to be out there, making a difference in the world. Not *stuck* dealing with stupid customers at a restaurant."

"Yes, I understand all that, but why does it have to be you? There are plenty of men already doing this kind of thing. Let *them* take the risks."

"That's exactly the point: *Men.* It's one of the only jobs left in this country that has a *No Women Policy.* It's dated *and* sexist and now *I've* changed that. *Me.* Your daughter. All by myself. And you were the one who said that I should write to the government. You're the one who taught me to fight for what I believe in. *You.*"

Dad shakes his head, clearly struggling to justify his actions. He reaches over to the centre of the table and takes the last slice of toast from the plate. "Look, Cath, I know what I said, but—"

"But nothing. It's obvious to me that you only encouraged me to write those letters because you thought that I wouldn't stand a chance. Well, now I've got through, and I've got the job and I plan on keeping it for as long as possible. And I plan on setting an example to all the other women out there who have to live in a world with *sexist pigs like you.*"

"Catherine!" Mum shouts from the sink. "Don't speak to your father like that. He's only saying what needs to be said."

"Okay, I'm sorry. I didn't mean to say that—but that's how it's coming across."

"Just because your dad thinks that something is dangerous," Mum continues, "doesn't make him sexist."

"Look, Cath," Dad says, his tone a little softer,

"I just want you to be safe. Your mother and I both do. I just happen to think that some jobs are better suited for men and some better suited for women. That's all. That's not sexist, it's just life. We're not all the same. We have lots of differences. And if you can't see that, well, then...more fool you."

Mum walks over to the table and stands behind Dad, her both hands on his shoulders, tea towel draped over her arm. "Look, I tell you what, Catherine, why don't you apply for something a little less controversial?"

"Like?" I ask patronisingly, knowing full well that she's just going to reel off a list of girlie jobs— like *nursing*.

Mum shrugs. "I don't know, maybe hairdresser, you know, something like that. *Or beautician*. I mean there's good money in that if you get in with the right salon."

"I've *got* a job, thank you."

Dad takes a mouthful of toast and then speaks; his words muffled: "Being a Cleaner doesn't even pay that well."

"It's not about the money," I retort, "it's about

the job."

Dad swallows and then sighs. "Well, I think you're crazy. I really do. And you'll only end up changing your mind again."

"What's that supposed to mean?"

"Cath, you've gone through more career paths than I have—and I'm fifty-bloody-eight."

"I haven't had that many."

"*No?* You sure about that? What about wanting to be an English teacher?"

"So what? I was fifteen. I was just a stupid kid."

"Then it was a doctor."

"Paramedic, *actually*, Dad."

"Okay, paramedic then. Same thing."

"It's not the same thing, and I only abandoned that because they were only recruiting in London. Remember? And you were the one who talked me out of it. You said that I'd hate living in such a big, dangerous city."

"Can't remember saying that."

I clench my fists under the table, seething with frustration. "*Typical*—selective memory as usual."

"Oh yeah, and then of course it was the Navy."

"What, so you want me to go off and fight in some shit-hole country then?"

Dad shakes his head. "No, of course not. My point is: this Cleaner thing is just another one of your little ventures. In a month, you'll get bored, move on to some other career path, and then you'll be handing in your notice."

I snort, struggling to contain the outburst that's brewing inside. "You don't have much faith in me, do you?"

"It's not that, Cath. I do have faith in you. I think you're a smart girl, with a great future. I just don't want you to risk it on some flash-in-the-pan job that you think is glamorous, and important."

"It is important. *Very* important. In fact, I believe it's just as important, if not more so, than a teacher, a paramedic—even a frontline soldier. And yeah, maybe you're right—I haven't exactly followed through with my career paths. But that's only because *this* is my true calling. And now that it's in the palm of my hand, I'm not going to let it slip away. And that's that, Dad."

The kitchen falls uncomfortably silent for a full

minute.

He finishes what's left of his tea and leans back on his chair, his eyes locked onto mine. "Okay, Cath," he says with a beaten-down sigh. "If it's what you really want, then I suppose there's nothing we can do to talk you out of it."

"No, there isn't," I say firmly, shaking my head.

Dad moans loudly, clearly unable to add anything productive. "Just be careful, for Christ's sake."

Beth walks over from her pillow and rests her furry white head on my thigh. She knows when I'm pissed off or stressed out, even if I'm not screaming the place down. Must be a dog sixth-sense thing. Seeing those pitiful eyes always manages to calm me. "Don't worry, Dad," I say with a thin smile, stroking the top of Beth's soft head. "I'll be all right."

Mum walks over to me and kisses my cheek. "And make sure you don't get bitten. Those things are bloody vicious."

"Okay, Mum," I take her hand, beaming. "I'll try not to."

3

I pull up outside HQ, which, *fingers-crossed*, I'll be calling work in the next few days.

I sit and wait in the car for a minute or two. For some reason, I'm more nervous today than I was at the interview. Can't think why. Fitness is easily my best subject. I've already done all the hard work. So why the hell do I feel so anxious?

It's the other Cleaners, Cath. You're worried that they're going to laugh in your face when they meet you. You're worried that they're going to tell you that women shouldn't do this kind of job.

But this is exactly what I expected. As long as I do a good job and prove them wrong, they'll have to respect me. Maybe I'll get a bit of banter, a few practical jokes, I mean, they're *boys* for Christ's sake—that's what boys do.

I take a few deep breaths, check my hair in the rear-view mirror. I need a haircut. Not too short, though, just a little further up from my shoulders. I part my hairline with my fingers and notice that some of my roots are showing. I'll get that sorted next week. Don't want them seeing that I'm not a natural blonde. The last thing I need is them calling me *Ginge* for the next five years. No thank you.

I check my teeth and then climb out of the car, heading for the gates. I push them open and make my way towards the entrance. I see someone standing against the wall by the doors, smoking a cigarette. Haven't seen him before. He's a big guy, maybe six foot in his late forties, early fifties, quite chunky, like a rugby player, and close-shaved head. Looks like an ex-army type, and most definitely a Cleaner.

"Hi there," I say as I reach the doors, trying to seem polite, but casual. "How's things?"

"Fine," the man replies, as he flicks his cigarette onto the ground, then grinds it into the concrete with his leather boot. "You must be Catherine."

"Yeah, that's me. Nice to meet you." He shakes my hand—yet another tight, macho grip. *What the hell is wrong with these people?*

"Training day then?" he asks.

"Yeah."

"You fit?"

"Yeah, pretty fit. Well, hopefully," I stammer, nerves getting the better of me. "I've been training."

The man grabs his slightly swollen gut. "Well, the good news is, once you pass your fitness test, they'll never test you again. You can be as unfit and as fat as you want. Genius, isn't it?"

I chuckle. "Really? I thought we'd be tested every six months."

"*Hell no.* The last test I had was nearly fourteen years ago. It's ridiculous. But, I'm not complaining. Can't stand running. Strength training's fine, but my right knee's a little iffy."

"Yeah, mine too. Left one. Injured it a few years ago. Had to have surgery. It's fine now, though."

"Sounds nasty." He takes out another cigarette from his pack and puts it in his mouth. "Well, good luck in there, Cath. You're gonna need it."

"Thanks," I say with a thin smile. "Oh, sorry, I didn't catch your name."

"It's Andrew. Andrew Whitt."

"Nice to meet you, Andrew." I push the doors open.

"Yeah, you too."

He seems nice. Maybe I've underestimated these Cleaners. Maybe they're fine.

Walking down the corridor, I head towards Roger Davies' office. When I get there, I give the door a gentle tap and wait. After a few seconds, Roger comes to the door, his large frame almost filling the doorway.

"You made it then," he says. "No last minute change of heart?"

"No chance," I say with enthusiasm. "I'm raring to go, Roger."

"That's great, Catherine. How's that knee of yours? Do you think it'll give you any trouble on the run?"

I shake my head confidently. "Absolutely not. It's stronger than ever."

"*Excellent.*" He steps out of his office, pats me hard on my shoulder and starts to walk down the corridor. "Shall we get started then?" he asks, motioning with his head for me to follow.

"Sounds good," I reply, walking behind—trying to squash every last butterfly that's fluttering in my stomach.

* * *

It's started to rain and it's bitterly cold.

I'm hoping Roger will just pass me for the day with the weather so bad. But with all five Cleaners standing around Roger, thick jackets on, hoods up, big smiles spread across their faces (all except Andrew), I'm pretty sure that they prayed for rain to come, to make this ordeal even more arduous.

Standing in front of a chalked start-line, I can feel those stupid, annoying little butterflies again. Back from the dead.

"You ready, Catherine?" Roger asks, standing next to me, holding a stopwatch, his thumb grazing the start button.

"*Yep*," I say as the rain hammers against my head, running down my face like ice-cold sweat. "I'm ready."

He points at the five tarpaulin sacks to the left of me, each with a thick rope tied at the top. "Five sacks, weighing seventy kilos apiece. Five minutes to get them over to the other line," he points ahead. "It's twenty metres, so it's gonna be tough. It's not too late to back out now. No one would blame you."

Prick.

I glare down at the five sacks with determined eyes. *You can do this!*

I throw Roger a nod. "I'm ready. Let's get this over with."

"Good girl." He stands aside. "Grab the tied end of the first sack." I do as he says and hold the rope as tightly as possible, hands soaking, my grip slippery. "Ready? *On your mark. Get set... GO!*"

And I'm away.

The sack weighs a ton, but it's moving. *Thank God for that.* I'm halfway to the end and already my fingers are slipping. I swap hands and pull as hard as I can. Within seconds, I'm at the twenty-metre mark.

"Come on, Cath!" I hear Andrew shout from the start-line. "You're nearly there."

I sprint back and grab sack number two. By the third I can barely breathe; I'm exhausted. My knee is aching, my thighs and arms feel like lead, and even with the rain, the sweat is running into my eyes, burning.

Come on, Cath! You can do this! Just two to go.

"How much time left?" I shout to Roger, struggling to get my words out between wheezes.

"Two and a half minutes!" he replies. "You're doing well! Just keep pushing!"

The fourth one feels heavy. *Really* heavy. I have to work twice as hard just to get it moving, and I've swapped arms six times before I'm even halfway.

"Come on, Cath!" Andrew shouts. "It's nothing! Just a sack of feathers!"

It's definitely not a sack of feathers, but I appreciate the encouragement. I pull and pull, changing hands again and again, until my hands are numb from the pain and cold. *But I'm nearly there. Nearly home.* I try my best to ignore the searing pain in my knee. *Please let it hold out. Please let it get me to the end.*

I'm eating too much time. I can feel it. I'll never have enough to do the last one. Not in a million years.

I've fucked it up!

I get the fourth sack to the end and dart back

for the last sack. "How long left?"

"Forty-five seconds," Roger says. "It's gonna be tight."

I exhale loudly in disbelief and exhaustion. I grip the remaining sack with both hands and pull as hard as humanly possible. Even through the pain, through the tiredness, the sack gets moving straight away.

At the halfway point, I hear Roger screaming that there's just fifteen seconds left. The panic spurs me on and I slide the sack even faster across the drenched concrete. With both hands on the sack, I'm pulling backwards, blind, no way of knowing how far the line is.

"Come on, Cath!" Andrew shouts again. "Almost there!"

I can feel my hand slipping, I fight desperately to keep my grip but it's no use—I fly back onto the wet ground.

Without the sack.

Shit!

I scramble to my feet and clutch the top of it again. I'm just inches from the end.

I pull and pull but it just won't budge.

How much time do I have?

Come on, Cath—pull! You can do it!

It's moving again, but my hand is slipping.

Come on! So close!

I don't hear any voices of encouragement, all I hear is Dad telling me not to worry, that it just wasn't meant to be.

Well screw that! He's not gonna get the chance!

A last-second burst of adrenaline kicks in, blocking the pain in my knee, tightening my grip on the sack, and erasing Dad's voice from my head.

I'm close. I can feel it.

Pull!

You're almost there!

I drop to the floor in a puddle of rain as I pass the finish-line; lungs battling to function, knee throbbing, arms ready to fall off. But I don't care— I'm through. It's over.

Did I pass?

Roger kneels down beside me, stopwatch still in his hand. I look up at him, hoping to see a smile on his face. There isn't one. But what use would a smile be anyway? That could mean I've failed. I'm too drained even to ask, and his blank expression is making it impossible to guess.

"Come on, Roger," Andrew shouts, "stop torturing the girl, and tell her."

Roger shows me the time on the stopwatch. I can barely see the display through the rain, but it looks to me like four minutes and fifty-two seconds.

I gasp in elation.

Four minutes and fifty-two seconds!

"I passed?"

"By the skin of your teeth," Roger points out, and then takes my hand and pulls me up.

"Seriously?" I ask, unable to grasp the news, half-expecting him to tell me that it's all a joke.

Roger starts to walk back to the building. "Get an early night," he yells back without turning to look at me. "The real training begins nine o' clock sharp." He reaches the small side door to the building and then turns to me. "And don't be late. I hate tardiness."

"Well done, Cath," Andrew says. "That was impressive."

"Thanks. I still can't believe I actually did it. I thought I'd buggered it up on that last stretch."

"I think we all did," he says with a smile. "But you passed and that's all that matters. Woman or not, you've got some balls, Cath. I'll give you that."

"Thanks...I think?"

"Roger's right, though. Tomorrow the real training begins. You think you're ready?"

"I was *born* ready." Normally I'd cringe if I said something that cheesy out loud. But not today.

Today I'm another step closer to becoming a fully-fledged Cleaner.

And I couldn't be happier.

4

I've been sitting in the staff room, watching TV for the last hour. Roger told me to sit tight while he waits for Andrew to return from a callout. I don't mind chilling for a bit. After yesterday's training, my knee is aching. I had to put ice on it last night—I found it hard to get to sleep. Plus, I was tossing and turning, thinking about today. So far they've been pretty vague about most of the training. I mean, the health and safety video was pretty standard, but the sack pulling—*bloody hell*, that was one for the books. Never realised how hard pulling sacks could be. Still don't really know the relevance, though—certainly not with weights as heavy as seventy kilos. What am I, a bloody power-lifter?

I still can't quite believe I passed.

I got a few evil looks walking in this morning from one of the Cleaners. No *"Well done, Cath"*, or *"Good luck today"*—just a couple of nods, mixed in with a few expressionless faces.

What the hell did I expect from a bunch of Neanderthals?

Scanning the small room, I notice some of the posters on the walls. Typical boys club: *Pulp Fiction* on one wall, *Megan Fox* on the other, and a nude calendar hanging on the back of the door. Can't complain, though. I'm sure that if this place had just women, there'd be a few *Twilight* posters, and some nude fire-fighter calendar hung up somewhere.

The door opens and I turn to see two Cleaners, dressed in ordinary clothes; jeans, t-shirt, trainers. One with short blond hair, muscular frame, the other with dark hair, slightly overweight. Both in their late-thirties.

"You still here?" the blond one says, smirking. "Thought you'd quit."

"No, not yet," I say with a grin, trying to appear naïve to his obvious dig. "Can't get rid of me that easily."

The dark-haired Cleaner opens the fridge. He takes out a packet of ham, sniffs it, and then puts it back in. "You'll be gone after today," he says, smugly, taking out a carton of milk and swigging a mouthful. "And no offence, *Blondie*, but it's probably for the best."

47

"Oh, *yeah?*" I reply, still trying not to take the bait. "Why's that, then?"

"Because this is no place for a woman. And before you get on your high horse about *sexism in the workplace, blah, blah, blah,* I'm only stating a fact."

"Oh that's a *fact,* is it?" I say, unable to curb my sarcastic tone. "How do you work that one out?"

"Because it's not bloody fair that one of us will have to be lumbered with you. It's too dangerous. And I can tell you now, it won't be me, that's for sure."

"Or me," the blond one says, shaking his head. "No fucking chance."

"Well, I'm sorry you feel that way," I reply, swallowing the lump in my throat, "but no one's going to be *lumbered* with me. I'll be just as valuable to the team as anyone."

The blond one snorts. "You keep telling yourself that, love."

"You think I give a shit what you two think? What anyone thinks? I've got just as much right to be here as you."

"No, you bloody don't!" the dark-hair one

snaps, causing my entire body to tense up. "Look, I'm all for equal rights, but we're talking about risking the lives of men I've worked with for years—men with families, *kids*. And all because some *little girl* woke up one morning and decided to be a Cleaner? Well not on my watch. I've been here too long to let—"

Relief washes over me when the door opens, cutting his onslaught short.

"Everything all right in here?" Andrew asks as he enters the room, wearing most of his Cleaner gear—thick white overall up to his chin, leather boots, and gloves.

"Fine, Andy," the dark-haired *prick* replies. "We were just chatting with the newbie here."

"Yeah? Whatever they told you about me," Andrew says, turning in my direction, "it's a bloody lie."

I force a smile.

"Well, I'll see you both later," the blond *tosser* says. "Good luck today, *sweetheart*."

I don't retort as I watch the grinning *bastards* leave. Glancing down at my hand, I see it tremble

49

slightly. I take a few deep breaths, and smile at Andrew. "How was the job?" I ask him, as if the last few minutes hadn't happened.

"False alarm," Andrew replies, unzipping his suit from the top of his chest. "Right, I won't be long, Cath. Just give me five minutes to change and freshen up."

"Okay, Andrew," I say. "Do you need me to wait outside?"

"No, it's fine. I'll change in the toilet cubicle."

"Sorry about that. I bet you're used to changing in here."

Andrew smiles. "Well, yeah, but a change is always refreshing." He pulls the zip all the way down to his waist, revealing a white, sweaty vest. He cups his slightly flabby belly. "No one wants to see this—not even the guys."

I chuckle, and then watch as he disappears through a door to the side of me, praying that those two pricks have fucked off home.

* * *

After almost two days, I've finally managed to get my bearings on the place. Apart from Roger's office and the tiny staff room, the main attraction is the centre of the building: the training room. It's just a little bigger than a tennis court, with a large garage door at the far end. To the right of it are three metal containers, shaped like telephone boxes; there is a steel door with a large padlock at the front of each one. To the left of the garage door are six rubber dummies. And in the middle of the room is a thick white line, which stretches across the entire width of the floor.

In spite of a few nerves this morning, I've been looking forward to training today. I love this sort of thing. Learning how to assemble weapons, shooting targets. That was the best part of the Territorial Army. It wasn't quite frontline, but it was bloody good fun.

Andrew is standing next to me, wearing jeans and a white T-shirt. "Right then, Cath," he says, "follow me. Let's get you suited up."

"Great," I say, trying to hide my enthusiasm. He leads me over to the uniform section. I can see about a dozen helmets hanging on the wall, and below each hook is a bench with an assortment of white Cleaner suits piled up.

"Okay, Cath, as you've probably worked out, this is what we wear out in the field. These suits are completely *bite-proof* so you'll be pretty safe as long as you keep your helmet, gloves and boots on." He picks up a uniform, holds it shoulder height to inspect it, and then puts it back down on the bench. He does the same for the next. And the next, until finally handing me one. "Try this."

"Thanks," I say, taking it from him. "Shall I just slip it on over my clothes?"

"Yeah." He grabs another suit, checks the label at the top, and then steps into the all-in-one uniform. "Okay, so climb into it like you would an overall—you know, like you were about to paint the walls or something."

I put the suit on and then zip it up to my chin. It's a little baggy, but I can live with it.

From one of the hooks, Andrew pulls down, what looks like a black police vest. It has various sized pockets and pouches on the front, and the words: *Disease Control* written in small white letters along the left side. He hands it to me and I slip it over my chest like a waistcoat. "It should fit," Andrew says with confidence. "It's adjustable." He zips it up at the front and then pulls a thin strap on each side to tighten it. "You're right-handed, yeah?"

"That's right. Why?"

He picks up a thick strap from the bench and fastens one end to the bottom of the vest, and secures the other around my right thigh. "Well, this is for your gun holster. Can't have you reaching for the wrong side."

"Oh, right. Okay. Good to know," I say with quiet excitement at the prospect of shooting something.

"What size shoes are you?"

"Three."

His eyes widen in shock. "*Jesus.* That small?"

"Yeah. Well, you know what they say about women with small feet."

"No. What's that?"

"Small feet. Big brains."

Andrew smirks and then scans the boots,

picking up a few and then putting them back down. He then selects a pair from the end, holds them up, squints, and looks down at my feet. "They'll have to do for now. We can pick up a pair in town tomorrow."

"They'll be fine," I say, chirpily, taking the boots from him. "I'm not fussy." Sitting on the bench, I slip the boots on my feet. Just by the fact that I don't have to undo the laces is proof enough that these are a tad too big. I try to prod my toes and see how far off the end they are, but instead I feel the steel toecap. Never mind.

"Now, Cath, remember, these suits are more than just protection—they're a status. Police, firefighters, paramedics, absolutely anyone who sees us, in the uniforms, steps aside and lets us get on with our job."

"Really? Even the cops?"

"Yeah. *Especially* the cops. The last thing some police officer wants is to risk infection—no matter how keen, brave…or stupid. It's just not worth it. I mean, of course, we work *with* the police. They help put up barricades when the shit hits the fan, evacuate the public. We couldn't do our job without their help. But most of the time, they'd rather leave it to us—the canaries."

"Canaries?"

"It's just an expression, Cath. Nothing for you to worry about."

"What's it mean?"

"Well, if you must know, it refers to the old coal mines. Miners used to carry them down."

"A bird? Why?"

"Well, if the bird died of a toxic gas, like methane, then the miners knew it wasn't safe."

"*Oh, right*. I see. Learn something new every day."

"But, it *is* our job. Fire-fighters have to run into burning buildings. Politicians run the country. And we do… *this*."

"I suppose it can't be easy for anyone to risk something like that—especially if you don't have the right gear, the right training."

"And the right back up. The last thing you want is to get separated during an outbreak. I tell you, Cath, it sucks. It sucks ass *big time*. Don't let it happen to you."

"I won't."

Andrew nods. "Good." He picks up a pair of gloves and throws them to me. I catch one but drop the other. As I scoop up the one from the floor, I can almost hear his thoughts: *Typical girl—can't catch for shit!*

After we both slip our gloves on, he hands me a white helmet. It looks exactly like the ones riot police wear; motorbike-helmet fit, large transparent hard plastic visor, chinstrap. I put it on and Andrew tightens the strap. "Can you hear me?" I ask him, my words echoing inside the helmet.

Andrew nods. "Yeah. Loud and clear." He grabs a helmet of his own and then motions with his head for me to follow him. He takes me over to the other side of the room. There is a large metal cupboard against the wall, with a padlock clicked around the door latch. Andrew kneels down, takes hold of the padlock and enters the combination. Once the lock is off, he opens the cupboard. Inside, I see six guns, and several white boxes, most likely filled with tranqs.

Now we're talking!

"So how many tranquilisers will a gun hold?" I ask, as Andrew pulls out a gun and places it on top of the cupboard.

"Ten rounds." He takes out a tranq from the box and holds it up to show me. It's a dark shade of red, no bigger than a marble, with a sharp tip. "They're more like bullets than darts, so they'll cut through a Nec's skull like a peach. Once the tranq makes contact with the brain, it should sedate the rotter straight away. But some are stubborn little fuckers. That's why we've got to have a magazine of tranqs. There's not always time to reload. You've got to shoot fast, or get the fuck out of there."

"Shit. I didn't realise. Thought one was enough. How long will the effects last?"

Andrew shrugs. "Good question. Two, maybe three hours. Every Nec is different. Depends on how far gone they are. Some won't wake at all." He picks up a small steel box, no bigger than a blackboard eraser. "This is a magazine. Each one is preloaded with tranquilisers. We keep two spare magazines on us at all times, with another ten or so in the van." He holds up the magazine. "So, it just clips into the top of the gun like this," he secures it to the weapon, "and you're done. Locked and loaded."

I practise inserting the magazine in and out a few times, allowing my memory to absorb every inch of the gun. It reminds me a little of a paintball gun—but I keep the thought to myself.

"Okay," Andrew says, taking the gun from me, "now this is fully loaded. Ten may *seem* like a lot, but you'd be surprised how fast you'll use them up. And trying to clip a magazine on when there's five of them coming at you is pretty hard. That's why you always have back up. Going solo is *never* a good idea. You need one of you reloading, while the other is *un*loading. Do you understand?"

I nod. "Always stay together."

"Exactly. Good girl—you're learning." He makes his way towards the centre of the room. "Come with me."

I follow him.

We stop at the white line, facing the six lifelike dummies. They're about fifteen metres away, with muscular, skin-coloured rubber torsos attached to thick rounded bases. Each one has no arms or legs, just a lot of tiny holes across every inch of its body.

"See this white line?" Andrew asks, pointing down to the floor by our feet. "Never cross it. And I mean *never*. Always stay behind. The government's already on our backs about health and safety. None of us wants another inspection. So always stay safe—and stay behind the white line. Understand?"

I nod, like a schoolgirl listening to their teacher. "Yeah, of course. Stay behind the line. Got it."

"Good. So, Cath, you ever shot a gun before?"

"Yeah. I have. Back in the Territorial Army."

"Okay, well these shouldn't be too much of a problem for you then. They're a little heavier than a handgun, but much lighter than a rifle. They could be a little lighter, but, you know, budget cuts and all that bullshit." He puts his left foot forward, lifts the gun up to shoulder height. "Okay, so you wanna hold this thing like you would a rifle, keep it close to your shoulder, look down the sight at the top. And then *squeeeeeeze* the trigger gently. There's virtually no kickback, so don't worry about bruising your collarbone." He puts the gun into position, aims it towards the dummy, and pulls the trigger. I hear a faint thud as the tranq hits the rubber man, just above its nose.

"Nice shot," I say, excitement in my tone. "Right in the head."

"Always aim for the brain, Cath. Otherwise the tranq will have no effect."

"Of course," I give him a cheeky, excited grin. "So, can I have a shot then?"

Andrew looks down at me, his eyes suggesting that I'm probably the last person he should give a loaded weapon. "*You're* keen," he says.

"Just eager to learn, that's all."

He hands me the gun, points at the dummy, and then stands to one side. "Okay, Cath. Let's see what you've got."

One foot in front of the other, I put the gun up to my shoulder.

"Just line up the sight," Andrew says, "and then *squeeeeeeze* the trigger."

Closing one eye, I pull the trigger softly and feel a slight jolt when the tranq leaves the weapon. I lift up the visor to see where it hit.

"Not bad, Cath. Not bad at all."

"Where did it hit? Couldn't see."

"You hit his nose. That's amazing. Well done. You've got a bloody good aim, Cath. And it's hard first time, even with a little experience under your belt. Most people struggle with the helmet on. So hats off to you, Cath. Good job."

Beaming, I pull down the visor again. "Let's go again."

5

After lunch, I meet Andrew back at the training room. This time Roger's with him, plus another Cleaner, all three in full-gear. Don't know if I've seen this other guy before. Can't tell with the helmet obscuring his features. Probably have, though. One of the guys from yesterday, sniggering from the side lines.

"Andrew tells me you have a great aim," Roger says, his tone brimming with cynicism. "Well done. You keep surprising me, Catherine."

"Thanks. I had a good teacher."

"I bet you did."

I scan the room, trying to guess what's next on the agenda. Can't see anything obvious, but the fact that Roger's here at least indicates that it's something important. *Or dangerous.*

"This is Darren," Roger says, pointing his hand in the Cleaner's direction. "He's just here to help keep you safe this afternoon."

"Hi, Darren," I say, offering my hand for him to shake, "pleased to meet you. Cath."

He shakes my hand. "Nice to meet you, Cath. You ready for this now?"

"I don't know yet. No one's told me what we're doing."

"Well, Cath," Darren says, "this is where the *real* training begins. This is what separates the men from the boys—so to speak."

I nod, my smile completely fake. "So should I get suited up for this part?"

Darren looks at Roger, and they both laugh. "I should *think* so," Darren replies, smugly.

Assholes.

* * *

Once I'm kitted up—gloves, boots, and helmet, Darren hands me a gun and escorts me over to the white line, this time facing the three metal containers, shaped like telephone boxes.

"Wait by the line," he instructs me, and then walks over to the first container and starts to unlock the thick, padlocked door.

Frowning in confusion, I turn back to see what

Roger and Andrew are doing. Roger is stood between the rubber dummies, gun in hand, aimed directly at the three containers. To my right, I see Andrew, on one knee, his gun aimed in the same direction. Turning back to Darren, I see that the padlock is off the first and second box, and now he's unlocking the third and final padlock. Once he's done, he jogs behind me to a small wooden desk. He crouches down next to it, his gun also aimed. He puts up a thumb to both Roger and Andrew (but not me); both men return the gesture and lock their focus back on their targets. Darren pulls out a small piece of plastic, which, from here, looks like a TV remote. He points it at the first container and then a large red light comes on at the top of it. I hear a loud click as the door opens on its own. Hand trembling as I point my gun towards it, I struggle to hold my aim as the sweat runs down my face; my heavy breathing amplified inside my helmet.

I know damn well what's about to come out of that box!

I wince when I see the male Nec bursting out, a black muzzle around his mouth, muting his vicious snarls; his skin a greenish shade of brown, his dead eyes grey, drained of life, bled of colour. My grip around the handle of the gun is tight and my heart is thrashing hard against my chest. I want to run but my legs are frozen solid. I can hear one of the guys yelling at me to shoot—to shoot the fucker in the head, but all I can do is stare as he stumbles towards me, dragging his withered ankle behind him.

I want to go home.

Back to Mum and Dad.

They were right—this was a terrible idea.

I should never have signed up.

I'm such an idiot.

Such an—

The Nec drops to the floor the instant I let go of the trigger.

Everything seems dreamlike. All the loud words of praise from the others are muffled by my own blurry thoughts. I don't even remember squeezing the trigger. I'm just about to take my visor off, run to the toilet and puke, when something catches my eye. The red light on top of the second container is glowing. So is the third one. *What the fuck?* Two more Necs, both male, both just as mouldy as the first, come storming out of their boxes, towards me. I can smell the decay as the first one gets just a few metres from me. I squeeze the trigger. I hit his chest! *Shit!* The Nec is close. I shoot again, this time missing him completely. *Can't aim*, my hands are shaking too much. He's too near.

I'm fucked!

He's gonna get me.

Oh shit!

Then all of a sudden the Nec drops, struck from the side of his head. Definitely wasn't me. Just as I line up the sight towards the third Nec, he's struck between the eyes, dropping to the floor, motionless.

I watch, in a daze as Roger grabs the feet of a sedated Nec and drags him back into the box. Andrew and Darren do the same for the other two. They slam the doors and click each padlock back on.

I yank off my helmet and drop it onto the floor, taking in the fresh air as if I've just been saved from drowning.

"Are you okay, Cath?" Andrew says as he walks

over to me, his eyes wide with worry. "Can you hear me?"

"*Yeah*," I reply, the haze fading. "I think so."

"You had me worried there for a second. Do you need to sit down?"

I nod. "Yeah. Okay. Thanks." He takes me over to the bench and sits me down. Exhaling, I run my hands through my sweat-soaked hair. Darren hands me some water in a paper cup. I manage a smile as I take it from him, swallowing its contents in record time.

"What happened?" I ask no one in particular.

"You choked," Darren answers, bluntly. "That's what happened. You shot the first square in the face, but the other two? Fuck knows what happened."

"Lay the hell off her, Da," Andrew interrupts. "This was her first time. What did you *think* would happen? She's not trained in this yet. Everyone chokes."

"Not me," he replies. "I didn't choke."

"Yeah, but you knew what you were getting yourself into. She didn't. No one told her what she was doing. She's barely had enough gun training, and we just threw her into the deep end. It's not bloody fair."

"Look, it's better that way," Roger says. "It lets us know what kind of a Cleaner she'll be—one that reacts quickly to danger, or one that falls apart after the first scare. I won't have her endangering the lives our men. Not while *I'm* in charge."

"That's bullshit, Roger!" Andrew snaps. "And you know it!"

"Watch your mouth, Andrew! Don't forget who you're talking to. This is a standard test, and since last year it's standard practise that anyone training for the job must be able to cope with any type of attack. It's the rules. I didn't make them. You know that as well as I do."

"Look, guys," Darren steps in, "let's all just calm down now. She failed the test, and that's that." He turns his attention to me. "I'm sorry, Cath. I'm sure you're a lovely person, but it's over. This job is too dangerous to have someone who freezes at the first sign of trouble. It's not only dangerous for you, but for the lives of the other Cleaners."

My heart sinks. I want to stand up for myself, to fight my corner, but I have nothing. Nothing at all. They're right. I'm not fit to work here. Passing some fitness test has nothing to do with the job. *This is the job. This is the real test.* And I failed. *Miserably.* "It's all right," I say, my voice low, deflated. "I understand. I fucked up. I'm sorry. I don't know why. I thought I could do it, but I just froze. Maybe if I could have a few more tries. You know, just a little more practise."

Roger shakes his head. "I'm sorry, Cath, that's it. There's no second chances. This is elimination training. One strike and you're out."

If my nerves weren't shattered, if my body wasn't drained of any sort of spark, I might muster up the strength to punch the bald bastard in the nose, tell him where he can stick his stupid job.

But he's right. And he doesn't deserve it.

The only person who needs a punch is me.

Roger offers his hand for me to shake it. "Unlucky, Cath. Better luck next time, yeah?"

I pause for a moment, but then reluctantly shake his gloved hand. "Okay, Roger. Thanks for the opportunity."

"No problem. Pop off your suit and I'll meet you in the staff room."

Andrew looks seething, so I smile thinly and give him one of my 'don't worry about it' shrugs. I then start to remove my suit.

The biggest surprise today wasn't the rancid Necs coming at me, nor was it the fact that I failed—there was always a chance that I wouldn't make the cut. The biggest shock is the fact that I haven't broken down in tears. Not one.

They'll probably come later.

6

It's 8:17 p.m.

I put my phone on silent the moment I left HQ. Didn't want to speak to any friends. All I've done since coming home is tell my parents the news of my failure, and listen to them struggle to find nice ways to say *I told you so*. But in the end, no matter how they dress it up, no matter how many sympathetic smiles I get, the bottom line is: they were right. Everyone was right. Everyone but me. Don't know what I was thinking.

I thought shooting one of those Necs would have been the highlight of the day, the highlight of the training. *My life*. Not some stupid sack-pulling race. I didn't even get the chance to celebrate taking the first one down with the tranq. I was too dazed for it to even register. And for all I know, it was just a fluke. I can hardly remember pulling the trigger. It's a good thing that Roger failed me. What possible use could I be in the field if I freeze at the first sign of trouble? Back when I was a little girl, I thought shooting Necs for a living would be the greatest and easiest job in the world.

Shit, was *I* wrong.

Greatest? *Maybe*. Easiest? Definitely not.

But to rub salt in the wound, I've got to go crawling back to the restaurant to get my old job back. Why on the earth did I have to quit? I should have just taken a few days off, done the training, and then told them where to go. At least then I wouldn't have to go back there, tail between my legs, with everyone knowing that I failed miserably.

I was so sure that I'd pass. So confident in my abilities.

Silly little girl.

I hear a gentle tap on my bedroom door. "Come in," I call out.

The door slowly opens and in walks Dad, dressed in his shirt and tie, a compassionate smile on his mouth. "How are you feeling, Angel? Any better?"

I shuffle up into a sitting position. "I'm okay, Dad. Just dreading going back to that restaurant."

Dad sits on the end of the bed. "Do you think your boss will take you back?"

I shrug. "Hopefully. I've worked there long enough. Just not looking forward to seeing that *smug* look on his fat face, that's all."

"Well, maybe you should hold out for something else. Something better."

"No, it's all right, Dad. Don't want to stay in bed for the next two weeks, moping about some job I didn't get. Got to keep earning. Pay my way and all that."

"That's the spirit, Cath. And look, maybe you could apply to the police instead."

"I've already looked into it. They're not recruiting until next year. Not in Wales, anyway. And I don't fancy moving all the way to Birmingham on my own. It's not for me. I'm a Welsh Lass through and through."

Dad beams. "That's good to know. I'd hate for you to leave us. Your Mum and I kinda like having you around."

"Thanks, Dad."

He pats my leg. "You sure you're all right?"

"I'm fine. Just need a day or two to get back on track. Who needs that stupid job anyway? Bunch of

Neanderthal, sexist assholes. *Good riddance.*"

"Yeah. Life's too short to dwell." Dad gets up off the bed. "Right, well, I'm off to do some paperwork. It's not quite as exciting as catching zombies for a living, but it suits me to the ground."

"They're called Necs, Dad," I correct him, chuckling. "Short for Necro-Morbus. Not zombies."

"Same bloody thing," he replies as he exits the room.

Zombie.

Never heard Dad refer to them as that before.

Sounds pretty stupid out loud.

* * *

Once I'm showered, teeth cleaned, I go back into my bedroom and pull out my hairdryer from my dresser. I sit in the chair and stare into the mirror as I dry my hair. Even though the steaming hot shower has woken me up, I can tell by my puffy, dark ringed eyes that I'm exhausted. Definitely need an early night.

Don't know how I'm going to face setting foot in that restaurant tomorrow. Maybe Dad's right. Maybe I should hold out for something better.

Once my hair is dry and brushed, I get up from the chair and walk over to my bedside table. I notice my phone, still on charge, still set to silent. Pulling the cable out of the socket, I see that I've had four text messages, two from Steph, one from my parents, and one from Rachel. Can't be bothered to read them right now. I know exactly what they all say: *'Hi Cath. How did it all go today? Did you pass? Have you taken out any Necs yet?'* Don't think I'm quite ready to tell them all about my disastrous failure. Not right now anyway. I also see that I have four missed calls: two from Dad and two from unfamiliar numbers. There's voicemail. I click the icon and put my mobile to speakerphone so I can finish dressing.

"Hi, Cath, it's your Dad. How did it go today? Did you knock 'em dead? No pun intended. Call us when you're done. Love you."

A second message comes through: *"Hi, Miss Woods. Did you know that you might be entitled to compensation? If you were miss-sold Payment Protection*

75

Insurance we can—" Don't fancy listening to another second of that shit so I quickly delete it.

The final message begins to play: "*Hi, Catherine, it's Roger. Roger Davies? Can you give me a quick call when you get this message? There are a couple of things I'd like to speak to you about. Thanks.*"

Intrigued, I dial the number. It rings for a few seconds before a voice comes through the speaker: "Hello. Roger Davies speaking."

"Hi, Roger, it's Catherine," I answer, trying to conceal the apprehension in my voice. "Sorry I missed your call; my phone's been on silent. Everything all right?"

"Yes, yes. Everything's fine, Cath." He clears his throat loudly. "Look, I'm sorry about today. I know things got a little heated between me and Andrew, which was unprofessional. Unfortunately, in a job like this, tempers can flare up, moods can swing, and disagreements are commonplace. But this is always the way with a team like the one we have."

"It's okay, Roger. I understand. You have a job to do—you've got to look out for the staff. I get that."

"Good, good. I'm glad. But, as Andrew pointed out, this job is a learning curve, and in spite of the rule book the government has set out, it *is* my ship. And as captain I do have a little power to do things in a way I see fit. So, I've spoken to Andrew, and he's agreed to let you shadow him for six months training. Out in the field."

What?

I'm nearly sick to my stomach when I hear his words.

Did I *actually* hear them? Or am I just half sleep?

"So, I know that three months is the standard probation period," he goes on, "but as a compromise I've had to increase it to six. I hope you can understand that, Cath. I mean, this wasn't an easy decision to make. It took a lot of ear bending, particularly from Andrew, but, well…what do you say? Are you in or out?"

If he could see the great big smile spread across my face like *The Joker*, he'd know my answer. "Of course I'm in, Roger. I'd love to. More than anything."

"That's great, Cath. Seven tomorrow morning.

Bright and early."

"No problem, Roger," I reply, trying to rein in my exhilaration. "I'll be there with bells on."

"Okay then, Cath. I'll be leaving you in the safe hands of Andrew. Don't worry, he may seem like a soft touch, but he's a tough Cleaner. Been at it even longer than I have. He'll be running you through the last of the training—gun practise, antiviral shots, muzzles—those sorts of things. If there're no call outs, I'll even get him to run you over to Romkirk furnace. You'll get to see how all this ends. Okay with you?"

"Sounds awesome, Roger. Looking forward to it. Thank you so much for the opportunity. I promise I won't let you down."

"I'm sure you'll do fine, Cath. Enjoy the rest of your evening and I'll see you in the morning."

"Okay, Roger. And thanks again."

"Bye."

I end the call and then sit on the edge of the bed. Need a moment to absorb the crazy, unprecedented news. It's like Christmas, Easter, my birthday, and quitting my shitty job at the restaurant, all rolled into one.

Leaping up from the bed, I grab my phone, unplug the charger and slip it into my handbag. I just want to scream the news from the landing, down to Mum and Dad like a kid excited about a brand new toy. But I don't even know how they'd take the news. They want me to be happy—that much I'm certain of. But actually getting to be a Cleaner—full-time? Who knows?

But more importantly—who cares?

I'm going to be a Cleaner!

Me!

The girl Suzy May used to pick on!

I ain't such a pushover now!

The dead had better stay dead, because Catherine Woods is coming for blood!

7

I've been in the staff room since 6:45 a.m., and the only person I've seen so far is Darren, coming off a nightshift—looking extremely tired and pissed off. I gave him a polite smile, and in fairness he did return one, but it definitely looked strained. No sign of Andrew though. Roger let me in earlier. He gave me an ID badge, told me to wear it on my chest with pride, and for me *not* to lose it. I look a little shell-shocked in the photo—but who the hell cares?

I'm a Cleaner!

It's almost eight by the time Andrew walks through the door, wearing just his grey joggers and a T-shirt, and carrying a metal briefcase. "Hi, Cath," he says, seeming all flustered and rushed, like someone just dragged him out of bed. "Sorry I'm late. We got a late call last night. False alarm though. Just some crazy tramp fucked up on God-knows-what, trying to bite chunks off another lowlife."

"Really? Another one. I guess you get a lot then."

"Yeah. At least four or five a week. It's the

80

police and nurses, see. They don't like to chance anything. Once they spot someone suspected of being infected, they report them. They've got to. It's too much of a risk to the public to take chances. That's why we've managed to stop Necro-Morbus becoming an epidemic. It hasn't been easy, though, I can tell you."

"I bet."

Andrew starts to pour himself a coffee from the jug by the projector screen. "Want one?"

"No thanks," I reply, shaking my head. "Still got one."

He sits on one of the chairs, just in front of me, takes a long sip of his coffee and then sets it down on the table.

"Any near-misses?" I ask.

"What do you mean? Like bites? *Hell yeah.*"

"No, I mean near-misses with, you know, the virus spreading into one of the cities. I haven't heard of any, but I know what the government is like. They only tell you half the story."

"We've had a few. There was the stadium incident a few years back. But that was all over the news."

"Oh yeah. I think I remember reading about that."

"*Yep*, that was a close one. But other than that, we've been doing a pretty good job keeping it back." He takes a gulp of coffee and then lifts up the briefcase and places it on the table.

"What's that?" I ask.

"Antiviral," he replies, unclipping the catches at the front, and then opening up the case, revealing a blue injection gun and six glass bottles of clear liquid, each roughly the size of a shot-glass. "These have been around for about six years. You seen one before?"

I shake my head. "Only on TV. No one I know has ever had to have one."

"Count yourself lucky, then."

"Do they actually work? I read somewhere that unless you take a shot within a few seconds of infection, they're pretty much useless. Is that true?"

Andrew shrugs. "Maybe. Depends."

"On what?"

"On the host. For some, they can work for a

while after getting bitten, and some, well, they don't even work within seconds of infection. Everyone's different, Cath. It's the same with Necs. Some walk, some stumble, some sprint, and some don't even wake. It's hit or miss. All depends on the person."

"Couldn't we just take a huge dose before we go into a hot zone, you know, as a precaution?"

"No, that would be a total waste. And they're bloody expensive. They're only effective after Necro-Morbus is in the bloodstream."

"Oh, right. So are these antivirals for the people we help, or are they for us?"

"Both, I suppose. For you, mainly. You have to think of the bigger picture. You're no good to anyone as a Nec, so you have to stay healthy, stay clean. Otherwise, all those people, all those helpless children, old folks, relying on your skills to get them out, to clear the streets of Necs, are all screwed. And that's the hard truth, Cath. It's just us between them and the dead. And we can never fail—no matter how little staff we have, how underfunded we are. We still have to fight. Do you understand?"

"Yes. Totally. So how many of those shots can

we carry?"

"You'll always have one injection gun strapped to your vest and one antiviral bottle, sealed in a protective case. We always keep spares in the back of the van. Just in case. You can inject one of these into almost any muscle. Doesn't have to be near the bite. They're pretty straightforward to use." He slurps the last of his coffee, gets up and pours himself another. He then turns to me, leaning up against the table. "Okay, Cath," he digs into his pocket and pulls out a handful of long plastic strips, about twelve inches in length, and a black muzzle. Not the kind you'd strap onto a dangerous dog, more like the ones you'd find in some nasty sex dungeon—but without the *Pulp Fiction* snooker ball to bite down on. It's just a thick piece of leather-looking fabric, which wraps around the mouth and chin.

I see an image of those *decomposing Necs* from yesterday, coming at me; their mouths covered with the same muzzle.

Gross.

He holds up the plastic strips. "I take it you've

seen these before."

"Yeah. They look like cable ties."

"Gold star. You're right; they are cable ties. No different from those used at home. They're very strong and they go around the wrist and ankle of a sedated Nec. Make sure you pull them as tight as you can, until the plastic *really* digs into the skin."

A vision of rotten flesh painfully shifting off wrist-bone fills my mind. Like tearing fried chicken apart with oily fingers.

"Do you think they feel it?" I ask.

Andrew smirks. "What—pain? Of course they don't."

"How would anyone know that for sure?"

"Because they're dead—that's why. They don't feel anything. How could they? They don't breathe, blood doesn't pump around their bodies, and they don't feel or care about anything. They're just walking, biting, viruses. Nothing more. Nothing less. Never forget that or this job will seriously fuck up that head of yours. Trust me. I know. I've been there."

"No, I know that. It's just—"

"It's just that every so often you read some bullshit in the newspaper about Necs not actually being dead. Am I right?"

"Well, I suppose so."

"Please tell me you don't believe that, Cath. If you feel that way, I suggest you call it a day right now—*before* you walk into a houseful of Necs feeding on a bunch of kids."

"No, it's not what I'm saying. I know they're dead. And I know that it's just a virus that's taken over a dead host. I know all that, I promise. But no one really knows what it feels like to be dead. How could they?"

"Nothing *dead* feels anything. It's over. There's no emotion. No love. No anger. Just some leftover instinct to eat. That's it."

Why can't I just keep my big mouth shut? I can tell that I'm pissing the guy off. I've only just got here and already I'm giving my opinions to a man who clearly isn't interested.

Shut the fuck up, Cath!

"Okay, the muzzle," Andrew begins, clearly desperate to change the subject. "This little piece of leather is probably the most important thing a Cleaner can have on him—*after* the tranq gun, of course. But a tranq will only last so long. Get this thing around a Nec's mouth, and the smelly bastard ain't tucking into anyone, *that's* for damn sure. It's very simple. You take the strap. Place the leather pouch directly over the Nec's mouth—preferably when it's comatose—and then fasten one strap over the top of his head, and the other around the sides." He shows me the two buckles at the end of each strap. "Just tighten these at the back of the head like you would a belt. Easy."

"Can we reuse them?"

Andrew shakes his head. "Once these are strapped onto a Nec, then that's it. They're shipped over to Romkirk for burning. It's too dangerous to open the body bags and remove the muzzles. A lot of the times, the sedation has worn off by the time they get there. It's only the cable ties, body bags," he lifts the muzzle up and jiggles it, "and these babies, keeping the Necs from chewing down on some poor Burner's throat." He hands me the muzzle and smiles. "You wanna try it out?"

I frown with puzzlement. "What? On me?"

Andrew sniggers. "*No.* Not on you. A bloody Nec, of course."

"Oh, right," I reply, relieved.

He makes his way towards the door, motioning with his head for me to follow. "Right, Cath, let's get to the training room. We've got lots more to get through today." He turns to me, and grins. "You ready to shoot some zombies?"

I smile back. "*Damn right.*"

8

Sunday the 22nd of February 2015. 2:16 p.m.—a day that will be remembered for many years to come.

The day of my very first call-out.

Nerves have slowly got the better of me. I'm trying my utmost to swallow them down, but it's hard. I'd like to think that it's just pure excitement, a surge of adrenaline—but I know it's not. Andrew's a little worried, too; I can see it in his eyes.

But I won't let him down.

I can't.

"So how far's this farm house?" I ask, holding onto the sides of my seat as he speeds down one of the narrowest country lanes I've ever seen.

"It's not that far. Maybe another fifteen miles or so. It's just outside Port Talbot. I had a feeling we'd be back up this neck of the woods."

"What do you mean?"

"Some teacher got infected nearby. She said she'd caught it off her grandfather over in some nursing house in Newport. We did our usual clean up, took down the infected, bagged them up. But I had one of those feelings that something wasn't right. It was just…*too* easy."

"So what happened with the nursing home?"

"It had to be shut down."

"The whole place?"

"*Yep.*"

"For how long?"

My entire body flies over towards my door as he burns around another bend.

"Not sure how long," Andrew replies, his face calm and collected, as if he was leisurely driving down the countryside with his family. "Maybe a few months."

"So what happened to the old people?"

Andrew shrugs. "Not sure. Probably re-homed temporarily until the place is properly decontaminated. All that shit, piss, blood, needles. Government can't risk any further infection."

I snort. "You know, I thought I knew everything about being a Cleaner. I really did. But there's so much to learn."

"You'll get used to it, Cath. Today's gonna be a breeze. This farmhouse is in the middle of nowhere.

Just how I like it. No other people for miles. So there's very little chance of any hordes of Necs coming at us."

"You think?"

"Absolutely! If you didn't get the job, I'd probably have gone on my own."

"Really? On your own?"

"Yeah. I mean, you're not supposed to, but Roger's cool like that. Well, if he knows that it's only a small thing like a farmhouse."

"Oh right, I see. So you reckon this'll be a walk in the park then?"

"Of course, Cath. Don't worry about it. You'll be fine. All I need you to do today is watch and learn. And if you can, cover my ass just in case. That's all. No one's expecting you to take down an army of rotters. So try and rein in those nerves, all right?"

I nod and smile, trying to show him *convincingly* that I'm calm, in control, without the flutter of a single butterfly.

But I'm far from calm.

And I'm positive Andrew knows it.

"Do your parents know you're on a call-out today?" he asks as he turns another corner, almost clipping a grass bank.

"No. They'll be stressing out all day. Especially Dad. They think I'm just watching instructional videos."

Andrew chuckles. "Probably for the best. Last thing you want is family worrying."

"Yeah—my thoughts exactly." I close my eyes for a second when we narrowly miss a passing tractor. "So how about *your* family? Do they still worry about you?"

Andrew doesn't answer. Can't tell if he's just concentrating on the lorry up ahead, or that I've said something out of turn.

"It's just me now," he finally replies.

"Sorry. I didn't mean to pry."

"*No, no.* It's fine, Cath. Fran and me have been divorced for about fourteen years now. After we lost Tessa, *well...*things just weren't the same."

"I'm *so* sorry."

"It's all right. It was a long time ago. Fran and me still talk occasionally—not as much as we used

92

to, though. You lose a child; you lose a part of *you*. I think that was the part that was missing from our marriage." He shrugs his shoulders. "It's just life, I guess. Sometimes it's great. Other times it's horse shit."

"So what happened to your little girl?" I ask, regretting the question the moment it leaves my lips. "*Sorry*. It's none of my business."

"It's fine. I don't mind talking about it. I've repressed it long enough. I've learned the hard way that bottling things up is stupid. Tessa was just seven years old, and I'd left the back door open; I'd been in and out of the house all day trying to finish off the garden. That summer had been a washout, so it was the only day I had to mow the lawn. I had no idea there'd been an outbreak in town. I was in the shed when I heard the scream. I ran into the house and found this rotten bastard digging his teeth into Tessa's leg."

"*Oh my God*. I'm so sorry." I swallow hard. "That's awful, Andrew."

"*Yep*. Pretty shit. I had to smash its brain to mush, right in front of my little girl. There was nothing anyone could do for her. Back then, there was no antiviral. It was only a matter of time before…"

I'm lost for words. Why couldn't I have kept my big mouth shut? Why do I always have to keep digging?

Nice one, Cath!

"That's why I applied for the job," Andrew continues. "It was the only way I could process what'd happened. I thought if I could kill as many as possible, then maybe I'd spare some other family the same fate." He shrugs again. "Something like that."

I wish I could think of something wonderful and useful to say, but I can't. I've got nothing. Instead, I just sit back, eyes on the road ahead, and promise never to open my big trap again.

* * *

After another few miles of tearing down deserted lanes, I start to feel a little queasy, as if I've just spent an hour on a rollercoaster. Got to take my mind off the road. "I never got the chance to thank you."

"For what?"

"For talking Roger into letting me keep the job."

"Don't worry about it. He's a good boss, but that doesn't stop him acting like a prick sometimes. He just doesn't see what I see. Not yet anyway."

"What do *you* see?"

Andrew glances over at me, then his eyes quickly return to the road. "I see a hard worker— and a fighter."

"Really?" I ask, blushing.

"*Yeah*, I do. I've never seen anyone pull those sacks the way you did. I mean, yeah, most of the guys who go for this job make short work of them; half of them are ex-military, ex-cops, so they're used to handling that kind of weight. But you? Well, there's nothing of you and you *still* managed it. So, for me, that's all that matters: determination and guts. Yeah, you froze in the training room—*but who cares*. Every job is a learning curve. You're not expected to make a bloody *Big Mac* on your first day without being shown how. Do you know what I

95

mean?"

"Yeah, I suppose so."

"There's no question. And doing this job is not just about being strong; it's about moving people to safety. Out of their homes. In the middle of the night. Cleaners rely too often on the police to do the talking when it comes to reassuring people why their children are being shipped off. If that were me, if that were *my family*, I'd much rather some pleasant, calm, woman come to my door and tell me that everything is going to be all right. Not some muscle-bound brute, barking orders like he's still in the bloody army. You know what I'm saying?"

"Yeah, I do. I never thought of it like that. I had it in my mind that I had to be exactly like you guys."

"To a certain extent you do. You still have to be strong. You still have to be fast. *And* you still have to shoot straight. But there's a lot more to being a Cleaner. And you'll learn that soon enough."

"Thanks, Andrew. I'm sure you'll do a great job teaching me. I'm a fast learner."

"I bet you are."

The country road comes to a fork. Andrew

slams on the brakes and the van comes to an abrupt halt. Leaning forward over the dashboard, he hits a button on the Satnav.

"What's wrong?" I ask him. "We lost?"

Andrew squints at the tiny screen and then shakes his head. "No. Not yet. Just over shot the turning. Wanna make sure. Don't fancy turning up at the wrong bloody farm."

"Can I help?"

"No, it's okay. I'll just turn her around." He swings the van around with one spin of the wheel; the front of the vehicle hits the grass bank in the process, and then speeds off back in the previous direction.

It's at least another four miles before Andrew slams on the brakes again, and bombs it down a dirt track. Flickers of mud and manure cover the windscreen and bonnet. Thank God it's winter and my window is up.

Another mile or so later, I can finally see something in the distance. A farmhouse. Andrew slows the van; I watch as he scans the trees and fields around us, as if hunting for something. I can guess what he's looking for—and my stomach starts to churn at the thought of a Nec ambush.

What Andrew said earlier makes total sense: a farmhouse in the middle of nowhere has probably the lowest risk of an attack from multiple infected. Unless, of course, they're a bunch of crazed hillbillies, harbouring a family of fifteen Necs, made up of uncles, aunties, kids, grandkids, the lot. But the farmhouse is quite small. Really nice, in fact. Authentic thatched roof, white stone right out of a medieval movie. There's a small shed at the side of the house, a tractor parked in front of a giant barn, and a mud-soaked Land Rover parked up at the side of a large gas-tank. I inspect the field; can't see any animals. No cows. No sheep. Maybe it's too cold for them. They must be in the barn.

"Should we be wearing our helmets when we knock the door?" I ask, picking mine up from between my ankles.

Andrew shakes his head. "Not right away. Keep it with you until the door opens. And keep your gun holstered, too. The last thing we want to do is frighten the life out of these people. Scared people do all sorts of dump things. Let them see a human face first, and then we can put it on."

"Okay. Got you."

We pull up outside the house. Andrew motions with his head for me to follow him. Nervously climbing out of the van, stepping out onto the damp gravel, I pat myself down, making sure I'm fully-equipped: gun, spare tranqs, antiviral, suit zipped up to the top, gloves, boots. All there. I follow Andrew to the front door. Before he reaches it, the door opens. Standing in the doorway is a woman, early sixties, dressed in a pair of loose-fitting denim jeans, cream shirt, with a brown cardigan; her grey hair in disarray, like she's just rolled out of bed.

"Mrs Rosemont?" Andrew asks, his right arm concealing his gun holster.

"Yes, that's me," she replies, her voice hoarse and flustered. "Who are you? Where are the paramedics?"

"We're from Disease Control. I'm Andrew. Andrew Whitt." He points with his left thumb at me. "And this is my partner, Catherine Woods."

I give her a very unprofessional, childlike

wave—as if she's a friend I've spotted across the street.

"Why on earth would they send you? My husband just needs a doctor."

"Where's your husband now, Mrs Rosemont?" Andrew asks, brushing past her comment.

"He's inside."

"Is there anyone else in the house?"

"No, just Keith. Oh, and Genie of course."

"Who's Genie?"

"Our golden retriever. No one else."

"Have you been bitten?"

"By who?"

"Your husband. Have you come in contact with any of his blood?"

She shakes her head in protest, seeming disgusted by the very notion. "Absolutely not! He's fine. He just needs a doctor. I told you."

"What are his symptoms?"

"Just a bit under the weather. Coughing, high temperature, vomiting. Nothing out of the ordinary. Just a bug. Or maybe food poisoning."

"Had he been anywhere just before? Maybe

visiting someone?"

"Yes, to see his father."

"And where was that?"

"Well, the nursing home used to be over in Newport. Golden Meadows. But the place recently closed down for refurbishments, so they've shipped him over to one in Bristol."

"So that was last night, yes? When he came home?"

"Yes. Around six in the evening. I gave him some soup but he couldn't keep it down, so I sent him straight to bed."

"And what happened next? Did he wake all right? Was he aggressive at all to you? Anything unusual? Cursing perhaps?"

"Absolutely not! Keith would never use bad language. Certainly not in the house."

"How is he this morning?"

"I'm not sure. He's been asleep all day. That's why I called for an ambulance. Never seen him like this before. It's not like him to get sick. He's as tough as old boots. So I left him in the bedroom."

Andrew glances over to me, signalling with his

eyes that it's time to enter the house. My heart rate starts to increase. I battle hard not to let it, but the apprehension is overwhelming.

I can't freeze. I can't let Andrew down. One Nec or not, it's still dangerous no matter how many there are.

"Mrs Rosemont," Andrew says, his tone firm, filled with authority, "for your own safety, I'm going to have to ask you to wait outside while we examine your husband."

"For my own safety? What on earth are you talking about?"

I decide to step in, to show that I'm not just here for the ride, that I can actually contribute. "Mrs Rosemont," I say, softy, "it's safer that you stay outside. There's been a report of Necro-Morbus around here, so just as a precaution, we're going to take a look at your husband. It's probably a false alarm, but we need to be sure. We'll be five minutes, I promise. Is that okay?"

Mrs Rosemont shrugs stubbornly. "Well, I suppose." She then steps out of her house. "He's upstairs—last room at the end."

"Thanks," I say, smiling, ushering her over to the van. "He's in safe hands. You don't have to worry."

Andrew gives me a slight grin, clearly happy with my performance, and puts on his helmet. I return the grin and slip mine on too.

Now my heart is really racing!

Inside the house, Andrew pulls out his gun; he whispers for me to do the same. He then slowly closes the front door, and it quietly clicks shut. I wish he didn't have to close it, I wish we could leave it hanging wide open. The thought of not having a clear exit fills me with such dread, such claustrophobia. But I understand why. We have to contain him if he's turned. Can't have him running out of the house, out of sight. It's too dangerous.

"I want you to stay behind me—no matter what," Andrew whispers. "Only shoot if I give the order. Is that clear?"

"Crystal," I reply, pointing my gun straight ahead, desperately trying to stop my hand from quaking. Don't think Andrew's noticed. Have to keep it together.

Creeping down the hallway, Andrew pokes his head into the living room. The room is filled with old-fashioned, brown, flowery furniture and there's a large, swivel armchair positioned in front of the TV, which is on, with the volume a little too high. The foot of the low, narrow staircase is just opposite the living-room door. Andrew gestures for me to follow him up. Logic suggests that I stay downstairs, to cover all corners of the house. But I know he won't let me out of his sight. It's too risky. Certainly not on my first official day.

Each wooden step creaks loudly as we make our way up the stairs. I can feel my muscles tense up. I suppose that's normal. Even Andrew must feel a little anxious walking up these stairs, about to face a potential Nec. I take a glance at his arms as he points his gun out in front. Steady as a rock.

Then it's just me then.

At the top, there's a narrow corridor with two doors along the sides, and one at the far end. The first door is already open—it's the bathroom. Andrew edges inside. There's only room for one, so I hang back by the doorway. There's a bath, sink and toilet. No shower curtain for Mr Rosemont to hide behind. *Thank God.* I take a step backwards as Andrew exits the bathroom.

The second door is closed. Andrew grasps the handle. "Be ready, Cath."

I nod, gun pointed firmly at the door, ready to take down any Necs about to burst out.

The door opens, revealing a tiny box room. It's completely empty apart from a few boxes of junk, an ironing board propped up against the wall, and a chest of drawers with several golf trophies positioned neatly across the top.

"Last room," Andrew whispers as he slinks towards the third and final door.

Reaching the bedroom, the grip on my gun stiffens when I see that the door is slightly ajar. Andrew gives it a gentle prod and it slowly swings open, my shallow breathing saturating my helmet. *This is it. My first real clean up. I've made it. It's actually happening. I'm actually here.*

And I couldn't be more terrified.

Andrew's large frame fills the doorway, blocking my view of the room. I try to see past his wide shoulders, but all I can see is a darkened room. Andrew steps inside, unblocking my view. From the doorway, I see that the curtains are still closed but there's enough light coming in through from the landing to make out most of the room. There's a small wooden wardrobe to the left, and just under the window, a chest of drawers, identical to the one from the spare the room. At the centre of the room is a double bed. The quilt is ruffled high, with a stack of various-sized pillows piled up by the headboard; at least six. Andrew walks towards the bed, gun still aimed in front. "Mr Rosemont?" he quietly asks. "Are you awake? We're here to take you to the hospital."

No response.

"Mr Rosemont?" he repeats, this time a touch louder. "Can you hear me? My name is Andrew Whitt. I'm a paramedic. I'm here with my colleague to take you to the hospital."

Still no answer.

Using the tip of his gun, Andrew nudges the raised quilt, but the gun pushes the quilt all the way down to the mattress.

The bed is empty.

Shit.

Where the hell is Mr Rosemont?

Andrew whips the quilt completely off the bed to make sure. "We need to search this house fast," he says, his voice still low, filled with urgency.

He pushes past me, and I follow him down the corridor, back to the stairs. Slowly, we skulk down each step, both guns aimed, ready for a sudden attack. At the bottom, Andrew peeps quickly into the living room, but once again the room is clear. "Stay here," he orders. "I'm gonna check out the kitchen." I nod and watch as he makes his way down the hallway. The kitchen door is ajar, so he pushes it open with his shoulder. As soon as it opens I can see that the back door is hanging wide open.

"Shit!" Andrew shouts. "He's slipped out! You need to go out the front door now and check on the wife."

"Okay, I'm on it," I reply, my words broken by dread. Just as I head for the front door, something catches my eye in the living room. The swivel armchair is moving. "Andrew!" I shout over to him as he steps out the back door. He stops in his tracks and turns to me. I wave him over. In an instant he's next to me, so I point to the armchair. He sees it move. On closer inspection, I see a small pool of blood that's gathered on the arm and the cream carpet. Silently, we both walk into the living room, with me leading the way slightly. Andrew puts out his hand in front of my chest to stop me going any further.

"Mr Rosemont?" Andrew asks, calmly. "We're here to help."

No reply.

At the back of the armchair, we both lean forward to examine the state Mr Rosemont is in. From the rancid smell and the pool of blood, I'm guessing pretty bad.

But instead of seeing a man, riddled with infection, we see a dog, with half its stomach ripped open, blood clotting its cream fur, leaking over the chair. Its body is twitching, eyes half-shut, hanging onto what little life it has left.

As I turn to Andrew, my heart almost stops in

horror. I see an obese Mr Rosemont—wearing just blue pyjama bottoms—stumble into the living room, arms outstretched, his mouth open, his teeth dripping with blood.

"Andrew!" I scream at the top of my voice. "Look out!"

Andrew frantically turns, but it's too late—Mr Rosemont manages to knock him off balance. The two men drop to the floor with the Nec on top of Andrew. The Nec is heavy, his weight pinning Andrew to the carpet. The Nec's jaws are merely centimetres from Andrew's throat, snapping and growling like a starving beast. Hand still trembling, knees like jelly, I point my gun, aim it at the back of the Nec's head.

I squeeze the trigger.

The tranq disappears into the mess of greasy, grey hair at the back of his head. The sedated Nec falls still, and then slumps over Andrew's body. Racing over to them, I attempt to push him off Andrew. His weight has to be at least eighteen, twenty stone. My hands sink deep into the exposed fat on his back as I push as hard as I can. With the help of a crushed and almost suffocating Andrew, we managed to roll the Nec off, onto the carpet. I grasp Andrew's gloved hand and yank him up to his feet. He grabs the top of the armchair for support, gasping for air.

"You all right?" I ask.

He nods, and then lets out a small chuckle. "Fuck me he was fat. Almost crushed me to death."

I smile. Can't believe I'm able to. I can feel the adrenaline, surging through my body. I look down at my shaking hands, still holding onto the gun for dear life. "That was close."

"Tell me about it. Need a cigarette." He unclips a muzzle and two cable ties from his belt. "Nice work today. Great shot."

"Thanks. I was worried I'd freeze again."

"*I* wasn't. I knew you'd come through." He hands me the muzzle and ties. "You wanna do the honours?"

"No problem," I reply, with a glimmer of apprehension in my voice, wondering where the hell my enthusiasm went.

"You've got to practise, Cath. You might have

to do this in a hurry next time. So do it as fast as you can."

I nod, and then reluctantly walk over to Mr Rosemont and kneel down beside his motionless body. The sour stench of death invades my nostrils, making my eyes water, even with the helmet on. His eyes are closed but his mouth is hanging open. Dried blood is pasted to the sides, down his chin and neck. I can feel the nerves start to build again as I quickly place the muzzle over his mouth and chin. I have a horrifying image of his eyes suddenly springing open and his head lunging forward, and his snarling teeth taking a chunk out of my throat. So I hastily buckle up the back of the muzzle as tight as it can go and let out a long exhale of relief.

"Good girl. Now the limbs. Make sure they're tight now."

I pull the cable around his wrists and fasten it tight—so tight that the plastic cuts into his bloated flesh. For a moment, I feel bad for making him bleed. But he's dead—and from the smell, he has been for quite some time. I secure his ankles and stand up with quiet pride. Last thing anyone wants to see right now is a victory dance.

"So what happens now?"

"First, we call it in." He pulls up the visor on his helmet, unclips his walkie-talkie from his belt and holds it up to his mouth. "Come in, Control. This is Andrew Whitt, ID number: 2368. Over."

"*Hi, Andrew,*" a female voice replies from the speaker. "*What's the situation? Over.*"

"We've just finished up over here at Rosemont Farm. One Nec, detained. One female in need of testing. Over."

"*Roger that, Andrew. We'll have someone with you shortly. Over.*"

"Much appreciated. Over and out." He reattaches his walkie-talkie to his belt.

"How long is *shortly* meant to be?" I asked.

"Not long. They'll send someone from the nearest hospital. Disease Control has trained most of the paramedics. And the hospital's only a couple of miles from here."

"Why call them now? Why not before we got here?"

"Too many false alarms. And it's a safety issue.

Can't have paramedics under attack."

"Oh, right. I see."

"If Mrs Rosemont is clear, she'll need somewhere to stay. Maybe a relative, or a neighbour. Can you ask her while I secure the area and get this one bagged-up? You're probably better at that stuff than me."

"Okay. No problem. But what do we tell her about her husband?"

"We tell her the truth," he says, sternly. "We've got no choice. It's horrible, I know. But there's nothing else we can say."

"And the dog? What should we tell her?"

"The same. And they'll both need burning."

"I thought dogs couldn't get infected."

"They can't, but we'll still have to burn it, just in case."

I let out a slow sigh. "Poor woman. Lost everything in one sweep."

"I know. It's pretty grim. But you're a Cleaner now, Cath. You have a job to do. You have to put on a brave face and deal with it. No matter what."

"Yeah, I know. It's just gonna take a little

getting used to, that's all."

"*Yep*. But it does get easier. That much I can promise you." He pulls out a small plastic packet from his vest, around ten or twelve inches in height and width, and tears it open. He then unravels a compressed yellow-coloured, tarpaulin body bag, "Let's get him packed away then." He throws it over to me. "Gag 'em 'n bag 'em."

9

The back of the van is sealed off from the front by a metal wall, so I have no idea if Mr Rosemont is still sedated.

I've got to stop thinking of him as *Mr Rosemont*—especially since we're on our way to burn him.

According to Andrew, the nearest furnace is Romkirk, situated just outside Bristol. He tells me that there are eight furnaces in the UK: Bristol, North Wales, Birmingham, London, Sheffield, Edinburgh, and Belfast. Swansea used to have a furnace, when the outbreak first started, but the locals protested to having one so near the city centre. So when that finally closed, the Welsh government never got around to building one nearer. They thought Bristol was close enough.

Typical government.

Apart from a brief history lesson on British furnaces, the fifty-five-minute journey into Bristol has been pretty quiet. Not sure if it's just the effects of the adrenaline wearing off, the dreaded comedown, or something else. Maybe he's still a little sore from talking about his daughter. Should I ask him what's up? No, best let him be. For all I know this is how he is after every Nec drop-off.

To hell with it—I'll ask him. I'm his partner and it's my job to make sure he's all right—whether he likes it or not.

Please don't shout at me.

"Everything all right?" I ask him quietly.

Andrew doesn't answer right away, his eyes firmly on the road ahead. "I'm fine."

"You just seem a little quiet all of a sudden. Is there something I've done to piss you off?"

Andrew turns to me, frowning hard. "Absolutely not. You've been great today. Spot on. The way you took out that Nec, without any hesitation whatsoever. And the way you dealt with Mrs Rosemont—fantastic, Cath. I can't fault you."

"What's up then?"

He lets out a drawn out breath, and then shakes his head. "It's just me, Cath. I totally fucked up today."

"How do you work that one out?"

"I let that bloody Nec pin me to the floor. He could have killed me. Both of us."

"It wasn't your fault. He caught us off guard."

"*Exactly.* I should never have let some *stupid dog* distract me. I should have been watching the hallway, not ogling some animal."

"Well we're alive, aren't we? We've got the Nec safe in the back of the van." I give him a playful nudge. "And you've got me to watch your back. What more can you ask for?"

A small grin starts to form on his lips. "You're right. Thanks, Cath. You're gonna do well in this job. I can tell already." Andrew turns down a country road. "Now let's burn this fat fucker before the tranq wears off."

* * *

The sun has long since descended as we reach the gates of Romkirk Limited. It's smaller than I imagined it would be, no bigger than a school. Plain design—a single sign by the main entrance. Only one storey high, grey walls and a huge chimney at the side. Andrew flashes his ID badge to the security guard, a white barrier slowly lifts, and then we drive down a narrow road to the back; the sides of the van brushing past the bushes and low hanging trees. After about a hundred metres, we come to a stop outside a set of steel doors, with a security keypad on the right side. Being in such a restricted place really brings out the excited child in me—like I'm part of some covert operation or secret society, or I've somehow managed to wing a seat at the Prime Minister's table.

"Okay," Andrew says, shutting off the engine, and then unclipping his seatbelt, "let's get this over with. I hate these places. They stink. *Literally.*"

Unclipping my seatbelt too, I follow him out of the van. Walking up to the door, Andrew pushes a button on the security panel. I hear a faint buzzing sound coming from behind the steel doors. A few seconds later, a voice comes out of the tiny speaker. "Hi, guys. Be with you in just a second."

"Cheers, Rob."

The door opens shortly and a man steps out through the doors, wearing a thick brown apron and gloves that go all the way to his elbows, and a set of safety goggles hanging around his neck. "Hey, Andrew. How's it going?"

"Good, thanks, Rob. How's the family?"

"Great. You?"

"Not too bad, buddy. Not too bad."

"Just the one for me this evening then?"

"Yep. Just one."

"*Fantastic.* Just the way I like it."

Rob follows Andrew to the back of the van. "But he's a big bastard," Andrew points out, opening the doors.

Can't help but think that's a touch insensitive, but who am I to judge? Andrew's been at this job for years. Of course he's going to be desensitised. To him, it's just a slab of gone-off meat—but to me he's Keith Rosemont: husband, father, farmer, dog-lover.

Andrew climbs up onto the van, his weight bouncing the rear a little. "Sorry, Rob, I forgot to introduce my new partner: Catherine. She just started today. First Nec capture of many. And it was a *hell* of a catch."

"Nice to meet you, Cath," Rob says, removing his glove and shaking my hand. "This big guy looking after you, I hope?"

Andrew snorts. "More like the other way around, Rob. This bloody Nec had me pinned to the living-room floor, nearly crushed me to death. Lucky for me, Cath's a crack shot. Right in the back of his head."

Rob's eyebrows rise. "Really? Well done. It's more than I could cope with."

"Just luck really. Right place, right time."

Andrew starts to slide the collapsed stretcher out of the van. "She's just being modest, Rob. Don't let the blonde hair and pretty face fool you—she's a hard-ass this one."

Blushing, I take the end of the stretcher and we pull it out of the van, the steel legs extending automatically.

I hear the faint sound of movement coming from inside the body bag. "Do you hear something?"

Rob puts his ear to it. "Sounds like he's waking up."

"Jesus? Already?"

"Well, he was a big fella," Andrew says. "I'm surprised he didn't wake sooner."

We start to push the stretcher towards the building, Rob and I at the back, Andrew pulling from the front. "Fucking hell," Rob blurts out, "you weren't kidding when you said he was heavy."

"And there's a dog in there too," Andrew points out.

"A dog? What's a dog doing in there?"

"The guy tore it to shreds. Thought it was easier just to burn him with the Nec."

Rob rolls his eyes and chuckles. "It better be dead, Andrew."

"Of course he's dead," Andrew says, pushing the doors steel doors open with his ass. "*I think.*"

Rob shakes his head. "Very funny."

The furnace room is exactly as I imagined it would be: hot, grubby, dark grey walls—with a smell of burned meat and that rancid stench of death. It reminds me of my first dog when I was seven, when Dad found him dead in the garden. That smell is etched in my memory for life. Lined up neatly in a row are about fifteen or so empty stretchers. There's a small stool, a couple of spare aprons hanging up on wall hooks, and a shelf with several sets of safety goggles and gloves. But the main attraction to this dark, depressing room is positioned at the far end. The furnace. It's a massive contraption, about four metres in height and about the same in width. To the left side of the thick, steel furnace door is a dial and a large red button.

"Well, Cath," Rob says, his arms stretched out wide, as if about to give us the guided tour of his luxury penthouse, "this is the furnace. I spend most of my time in here, burning the dead. The rest of the building is pretty much off limits to us mere Burners. It's all offices and training rooms, and all that bullshit. But here is where the real magic happens."

I can't tell if he's being sarcastic, or if he really does love working in this dump. Personally, I couldn't think of anything worse. "Enjoy working here, Rob?"

"Well, it has its bad points—long, tedious hours, the smell, which I'm pretty sure you caught a whiff off when you walked in."

I smile and nod in agreement.

"But these furnaces are vital," Rob continues. "Just like your job. They're the backbone of keeping everyone safe from infection. Without these furnaces, we'd have no way to dispose of them. Guns certainly don't work, severing the head doesn't work. Burning them to nothing more than dust is the only effective way. And I'm glad I'm a part of it."

So he wasn't being sarcastic then.

"Thought it might be good if she watched you use the furnace. Give her a little insight into the entire process of disposal. Is that okay, Rob? I know you're pretty busy."

"No, it's fine," he replies. "Be happy to. Just make sure you both stay back. It gets pretty hot." He pushes Mr Rosemont over to the furnace doors. "Okay, Cath. The first thing we do here is get suited up." He lifts his safety goggles up and puts them over his eyes. "Goggles, gloves, and apron. At all times." Walking over to the furnace, he opens the steel door. He then slides out a large, gridded platform.

I can feel the heat blasting out even from here, causing me to shield my eyes with the palm of my hand. I watch as the body bag jerks up, as if he's desperate to get out. Rob doesn't flinch when he sees this. I guess he must be used to it by now.

Is that what's going to happen to me eventually? Is all this going to be nothing but a job?

"So now we get to the hard part of the job," Rob says, walking behind the body and placing his hands on it. "Pushing this big fella in." Struggling at first, he manages to roll Mr Rosemont onto the furnace platform, and then starts to push him into the fire.

"Need some help?" Andrew asks.

"No, it's fine. Best stay back. I'm used to it."

Once Mr Rosemont and Genie the dog are both in the furnace, Rob slams the door shut and twists the handle to lock it. "Hardest part is over," he says. "Now the easy part: burning him." He twists the dial at the side of the door. "Turn it to green. And then push the red button."

Once he pushes it, the furnace comes alive with

a roar, causing me to stand back even further.

"And that's how it's done," he says, proudly. "It's not rocket science, just hard graft. Two thousand degrees Fahrenheit and he's nothing more than dust." Removing his goggles and his gloves, he takes a seat on the stool and wipes his brow with his sleeve. "It's a dirty job…but someone's got to do it."

* * *

It's a two-hour drive back to Ammanford. Andrew's been driving all day so I've offered. I don't mind taking the wheel; it's kind of nice driving around in a van. Makes me feel big, powerful, like the bully of the road. I can see why there's such a stigma with white vans: *White-Van-Man*.

Turning to Andrew, I can see he's tired; his eyes are half-shut and he's quiet. Been a long day. Don't even know if we get paid overtime. Hope so—I was supposed to finish hours ago. Not that it bothers me. Well, not right now anyway. I'm sure I'll be moaning when the novelty wears off.

"So what did you do before all this?" I ask him. "The army?"

He doesn't answer. When I turn to him again, I can see that he's fast asleep; his head against the window, his arms crossed.

Smiling, I focus on the road. It's a long drive ahead, a lot of things flying through my mind. It's going to be tough sleeping tonight. I knew today was going to be a real eye-opener, but I never thought I'd experience so much in one day.

I'm sure tomorrow will be a little easier. First days are always the hardest.

* * *

Back home I'm greeted by Beth as soon as I enter the kitchen. She jumps up on me, her sharp claws catching the cotton of my coat. "Down girl," I whisper, not wanting to wake Mum and Dad. I sit down heavily on the chair. Beth rests her head on my thighs and I stroke it. She closes her eyes, clearly enjoying every moment of it. I smile at how cute she looks, how loyal and grateful she is. But then my smile disappears when I think of Genie and her insides pouring out of her torn stomach. It makes me gag, so I get up from the chair and pour myself a glass of water. I take a sip by the sink and hold onto the worktop, waiting for the nausea to pass. It doesn't, and I throw up. Beth starts to bark at my loud retching. *Please don't wake Mum and Dad.* Don't want them to worry about me. This is normal. Of course, I'm going to be a little freaked out after seeing something like that. Who wouldn't be? Doesn't mean I won't make a good Cleaner. It just means I'm human.

I swill out the sink, swallow down the rest of the water, and then exit the room.

Unable to look at my beloved dog.

10

Monday mornings still suck even without a weekend attached.

Didn't sleep a wink last night, apart from maybe an hour of two. Couldn't get the images of Mr Rosemont out of my head, and his poor wife.

The clock on my bedside table reads: 6:44 a.m. I close my eyes for a moment in disgust at how soon I've got to get up, and how completely shattered I am. *Please don't let today be too difficult.* Don't think my body and mind will take anything too tasking.

* * *

Once I'm showered, dressed, I head down to the kitchen for breakfast. Dad is sitting at the table eating cereal. Mum is standing by the worktop, buttering some toast.

"Morning, Angel," Dad says, chirpily. "How was your first day on the job?"

I sit down. "It was fine. Just going through some training tactics, watched a couple of videos.

Nothing special." Don't fancy going into the grisly details. Not yet anyway. Especially not after last night's puking incident. Not only is it embarrassing, but it would raise too many questions. Questions that I'm just not ready, nor in the mood to answer.

"Anything dangerous?" Mum asks, handing me two slices of toast on a small plate. "Did you see any of those Necs?"

"Thanks, Mum," I say as I take the plate from her. "No, nothing dangerous yet. It's too soon for all that. Just boring stuff."

Mum kisses the top of my head and then walks back over to the worktop. "That's good, love. Can't rush these things. That's how accidents happen."

"So what's your day like today?" Dad asks as I take a mouthful of toast. "You working?"

I chew my breakfast quickly and then answer. "Back in for ten today."

"You're a busy little girl," Dad says, taking a swig of his coffee. He then gets up off the chair. "Well, I'm off to work. I'll see you two later. Okay." He walks over to me and kisses me on the cheek. "You be careful today. Don't do anything stupid, and listen to that boss of yours."

"I will, Dad," I reply. "Don't worry. I'll just be shadowing him. Nothing too risky. I promise."

"Good girl," he says, and then walks over to Mum and kisses her on the lips. "See you later, love."

"See you later," Mum says, buttering another slice of toast.

* * *

The radio is on at full blast as I drive to work, trying to block out thoughts of yesterday. I'm annoyed with myself for feeling like this. On the one hand, I never thought I'd feel anything but pure excitement at the prospect of catching Necs for a living. On the other, I'm mad with myself for not expecting that I'd feel so apprehensive about returning to work. Surely every newbie gets a little shaky after a first day. I wouldn't be normal if it didn't have an effect on my mood.

Once HQ is in my sights, I can feel those bloody butterflies again, the same ones that showed up on the day of my interview. But these have teeth—the teeth of a hungry Nec, gnawing at the walls of my stomach, trying to burst out of my abdomen. I try my best to drown them with heavy intakes of air, breathed in through my open window.

I could just turn back, tell them I'm sick—*or just quit altogether.* No one would blame me. My parents would be over the moon. I could just go back to my old job, spend my days serving rude customers.

I could.

But I won't.

I didn't come this far just to throw in the towel now. All those letters just to get an interview. All my research, all my studying just to show the world that a woman can do this job just as well as a man. If I turn this car 'round before I've even made it two days out in the field, then I'm just a pathetic failure. To all these people I swore I'd help, all those families I vowed I'd keep safe from infection, from the dead. I could never live with myself if I didn't at least give it my best shot.

These other Cleaners would love to see me hand in my notice, they'd laugh in my face. But it won't happen. Not while I've still got some fight in me.

Catherine Woods is not a quitter!

The moment I pull into the grounds of HQ, I feel sick. Parking the car quickly, I hang my head out of the window, like a dog in need of fresh air. I hold this pose for maybe two or three minutes, taking in as much oxygen as my lungs will carry, until the nausea finally subsides and I once again feel human. Almost. The cold breeze feels nice against my face, almost sending me to sleep. But then the sound of the entrance doors opening with force, and a barrage of heavy boots and loud chatter pulls me out of my daze, and I open my eyes. I see Darren, Andrew, and three other Cleaners coming out of the building, all fully kitted, clearly ready to leave for a job. I quickly park my car and then climb out. "What's happening, Andrew?" I ask, walking over to them. "Everything all right?"

"Oh, good, you're here," Andrew says, sounding flustered and agitated. "We need to get you kitted up right now because we've got an urgent job to get to."

"What, all of us?"

"Yeah. *All* of us," Darren shouts over, climbing into a van with another Cleaner. "We need every man *and* woman, out. Andrew, get her ready and we'll meet you up there."

Andrew nods and puts up his thumb as two vans pull off out of the grounds.

We sprint inside to get me changed. Once I'm kitted up, he does a quick check to make sure I haven't forgotten anything.

As long as I've got my gun, that's the main thing.

We hop into the van and drive off. Andrew tells me that we're heading back to Bristol.

To a place called Crandale.

11

Driving through Bristol City Centre, everything seems as it should be: people dressed in business suits walking along the pavement, teenagers loitering outside shops and bus stops. And the roads are as busy as you'd expect them to be on a Monday afternoon.

Andrew's been quiet for most of the journey. He seems tense, worried. Which makes *me* worried. He says there's been an outbreak, which has spread across the whole of Crandale—an area of Bristol that covers several large streets, a church, a primary school, and a community centre. We've been called in to assist, even though this is out of our jurisdiction. Apparently, it's been contained. For now. Police blockades, the works. Nothing's getting in or out.

Except us.

As we approach Crandale, I see police lights flashing. Looks like one of the blockades. There is an array of police cars and a portable steel wall, about three metres high, stretched across the entire width of the road, and held in place by a flat metal base positioned on both sides. And parked next to each base is a white van with a police officer on the roof, both armed with what looks like a tranq gun, aimed directly behind it—two makeshift watchtowers. The sight terrifies and excites me in equal measures, like sitting on a rollercoaster, moments before the track descends.

Just as Andrew nears the parked police cars, a female officer steps out onto the road, in front of us, waving her hands to stop us. Andrew slows down to a stop. The officer walks around to Andrew's window; he pushes the button and the window slides down. He shows his ID badge.

"Hi sorry, guys," she says. She then shouts over to a male officer in front of us, his police car blocking our path. "Let 'em through, Chris!"

The other officer moves his car to the side to let us pass.

"Thanks, love," Andrew says. "Are all the walls in place?"

"Yeah. Most of them."

"What's that supposed to mean?"

"Well, we don't have enough for the back lanes, so we've got the riot police and vans blocking them. The lanes are fairly narrow, though—nothing's getting in or out."

Andrew sighs, shaking his head. "Typical." He starts to advance towards the steel wall.

"Good luck," she says as he retracts his window.

As we near the barricade, my lips dry, my heart racing, all I can think about is Mum and Dad, sat in work, thinking that I'm just in some training exercise, safe and sound.

Two police officers unhook the giant latch at the centre of the wall, and start to pull it open like a gate-on-wheels, splitting the structure in two, using the giant hinges attached to each base. As the wall slowly parts, it reveals nothing more than an empty, everyday street. Fixed to the front of the first house, I see a sign for Rose Avenue. I grip my door handle tightly, trying to hide my trembling hands from Andrew. But he hasn't noticed; his eyes are locked onto the road ahead.

From my window, I catch a glimpse of the officer as he holds the wall open. I can't tell if his calm, emotionless face tells me that everything will be all right—or that I'm never coming out of here alive. I try to read Andrew's expression, but it's impossible. He's got that built-in macho pride thing, the one that likes to show the world that nothing bothers him, that everything will be fine.

I'll get there soon.

I hear the steel wall slam shut behind us—and the rollercoaster finally descends into the unknown.

12

We drive slowly up Rose Avenue. The street is deserted. Silent. Eerie. Like it's the end of the world and every soul has either perished, or left the planet.

"So what happens now?" I ask Andrew.

"We need to get to the church at the top of Richmond, and meet up with the other Cleaners. It should be somewhere after this street."

"And then what?"

"Well, I'm not really sure, Cath. We'll have to go with the flow. If the infection *is* as big as they say, *then…*"

"Then 'what'?" I ask; my words lined with worry.

"Then we need to be ready for anything." He turns to me. "But don't worry. You'll be fine."

He tweaks the dial at the top of the walkie-talkie, and then fastens it to his vest.

"Where's *my* radio?" I ask.

"I'm sorry, Cath. This is the last one. Normally there's enough to go 'round, but three are still being repaired, and well, the other Cleaners have the rest.

But you won't need one, anyway. As long as you stick with me, nothing's gonna—"

"Look out!" I scream. There's a man standing in the middle of the road.

Andrew slams on the brakes, propelling us forward, stopped only by our seatbelts. But he's too late. The man clips the side of the bonnet and is flung onto the pavement, landing on his side, hard, just a metre or so from my door. Can't see if the man is still conscious; his head is facing away from us. I unclip my seatbelt and grab the door handle to go to the man.

"Stop, Cath!" Andrew orders.

I let go of the handle in fright, turning to Andrew.

"What the hell are you doing?" he asks. "You can't go running outside recklessly. He might be infected."

"But what if he's not? He might need our help."

Andrew lets out a slow sigh. "Put down your window halfway and then point your gun at him."

I do as he says, checking that my gun is loaded before I aim it through the opening. I already know it's loaded—I've checked *twice*—but I can't help myself. I somehow manage to hold the gun steady as I inspect the man for any movement. "I think we killed him."

"I doubt it. We only grazed him. He's probably unconscious."

"Should we call out to him? Try and get his attention? He might just be in a daze or something."

"No, too risky. We could end up drawing out a swarm."

"We can't just leave him there."

"Look, any other time and I would. But we've had fuck all Intel from the Bristol lot. We have no idea how many are infected. The place might be teeming with them. So we have to be cautious. At least until we get to the church and speak with the other Cleaners. They can fill us in on the extent of the outbreak. Then we can go back for him."

"But it's pretty big, right? I mean, all these streets closed off. That's pretty big."

"Yeah, it is. That's why we stay in the van until we have a strategy."

I give him a nervous stare, mixed in with a look

of disappointment that we're about to leave a potentially injured man on the pavement. Andrew spots this look.

"Fuck," he says under his breath. "All right, we'll check him out." He puts his helmet on, opens the door, and climbs out. "But stay in the bloody van. I mean it, Cath. Don't move a muscle. It's too risky."

I give him a nod.

Gun pointed in the direction of the man, Andrew moves slowly towards him. Just a foot or so away from him, he scans his surroundings, and using his right foot, he gives the man a gentle prod.

No response.

"Do you think he's dead?" I whisper.

Frowning, Andrew shushes me. But just as he does, the man begins to stir. I clench up, ready to fire a tranq into the back of his head.

Andrew steps away. "Hello? Are you all right?"

A deep, guttural moan comes from the man.

"Are you all right?" he asks again. "Have you been bitten?"

The man lets out another moan, this time much

141

louder, prompting Andrew to step back even further. Using the hard pavement as support, the man starts to push himself up, still with his back to us. He slowly starts to turn his head towards us. I see his dead, soulless eyes, his teeth, smothered with brown blood, his light-green flesh, drained of all warmth and life. The Nec doesn't have time to snarl, to attack. Andrew unloads a tranq into his forehead, dropping him instantly.

Pulling out a muzzle, Andrew straps it around the sedated Nec, and then secures his wrists and feet with the cable-ties. He doesn't bother with the body bag and stretcher. There's no time. Andrew just throws his arms under the Nec's armpits, and yanks him up off the concrete as if he was lifting nothing more than a drunken friend. He drags the Nec to the rear of the van, the back doors squeaking as they open. The van judders as the body is thrown inside. I'm half expecting Andrew to slam the doors in anger, pissed off that I practically guilt-tripped him into going outside. But he doesn't, he closes them softly, with just the small click of the lock. He's smarter than that. Smarter than *me*. He wouldn't risk drawing attention to us. He climbs back into his seat, closes the door, takes off his helmet, and continues up Rose Avenue.

"Close your window," he says, coldly.

I hold down the button with my thumb and the window automatically ascends. "Sorry, Andrew. I didn't mean to put you in danger."

"It's fine, Cath. Don't worry about it. We did need to check on him. It's our job. I just hate not knowing fuck all about a job. It's not the way I like to work. It's too dangerous. And where there's one Nec, there's usually a swarm just around the corner."

"Well, we're here now. We'll find out soon enough."

Andrew raises his eyebrows. "Yeah. Soon enough."

At the top of the street, we stop at the junction. Attached to a wall, there's a sign for Richmond. We check out the street up and down. I don't see any wandering Necs. A little further up I can see the church. Andrew sees it too so he sets off again, up the hill towards it, the van's engine struggling noisily in such a low gear. *Too noisy.* I can see Andrew's face recoil as he changes gear.

As we make our approach, I see another man hobbling towards us, his head slumped to one side. I can't be sure from here, but my hunch tells me that this man died some time ago. Andrew stops the van just outside the church gate, and pops his helmet back on. "Stay here," he orders as he climbs out, shutting the door behind him. He shoots the Nec and then disappears through the gate.

I try my very best to stay calm as I wait for his return. I put my helmet on just in case he doesn't come back, and I'm stuck out here on my own.

Don't be silly, Cath. He's only been gone ten seconds. What's the matter with you? Don't be so overdramatic.

When a minute passes, and he's still not back, I start to panic. I can't stop my pulse racing, my erratic breathing.

Maybe he's in trouble. Should I get out and look for him? What if he's—

My body jolts in fright when I hear the driver's door opening.

Relief washes over me when I see Andrew.

"Come on," he says, confidently. "It's safe. And take the keys with you. Can't risk some idiot stealing it."

"With all this going on? They'd have to be mad."

"Remember what I said at the farm? 'Scared people do dumb things'."

I climb out of the van, gun still firmly in my grip, and walk over to Andrew. "What's happening?"

"First, we need to get a muzzle on this Nec," Andrew says, pointing to the man on the floor. "And then we drag him, and the other Nec, into the church."

"Okay. Do you want *me* to secure this one?" I ask, pointing to the newly sedated Nec, lying on the pavement.

"Yeah. If you can. But be quick, Cath. I don't wanna be out here any longer than we have to."

"No worries."

There's plenty to worry about.

Kneeling down, I unclip a muzzle from my belt and place it over the Nec's mouth before I even give myself a chance to freak out, to picture the Nec waking and biting me. I fasten the back buckle in record speed. By the time I've tied his limbs, Andrew has pulled the first Nec off the van and has started to drag him by the legs, through the gates, into the church grounds. "Follow me, Cath," Andrew says, struggling to speak with the weight of the Nec. "I'm sure you'll manage. Yours doesn't look that heavy."

"Okay." Grabbing his ankles, I start to pull him towards the gates. He weighs an absolute ton, but after that awful sack-pulling challenge, one Nec shouldn't be that much of a problem.

Inside the grounds, I follow Andrew up a narrow path, through an old, clearly disused graveyard. Couldn't have found a more fitting place to be dragging a corpse. The route up to the church is steep, and the concrete is broken and rough. I have to stop three times before I'm even halfway up. The church is as ancient and neglected as the graves that surround it. There's no way in the world that anyone still uses this place for worship. It's a huge building—beautiful, in fact—with stained-glass windows darkened by dust and decay. Most of the natural grey stonework is cracked, either from wear-and-tear or vandalism, and vines climb its walls like blood vessels.

Reaching the top of the path, we come to a corner. I follow Andrew around it and I see the church entrance, and a set of huge wooden doors, once again bruised and battered like the rest the place. *I'm never getting married in one of these things. Way too depressing.*

And when I drag the man inside, and see the mass of sedated Necs all around me, I find yet another reason never to get married in a church.

Gasping in horror, I drop the Nec's legs, and go to place a hand over my mouth, only to find my visor instead. I want to scream but can't; my mouth is too dry. My vocals have seized.

Nearly every inch of the place, every pew, every space on the cold stone floor, is occupied by captured Necs. There must be at least seventy. *Maybe more.* Half sealed in yellow body bags, while others are loose, limbs tied, mouths muzzled. Scanning in revulsion, I spot a few squirming—

147

sedation clearly worn off. The image is dismaying—*disturbing*—to see so many, so close. It's overwhelming.

"Don't panic, Cath," Andrew says as if I've merely walked through a cobweb. "You're safe. They ain't going anywhere."

When the walls stop closing in on me, when the tunnel vision starts to fade, when my mind begins to process what I'm witnessing, I manage to squeeze a sentence out. "What the fuck is this?"

"It's a morning's worth of work," a man says, from the direction of the nave, his voice echoing around the crumbling walls.

As he approaches, I can see that he's a Cleaner, his helmet under his left arm. Surely the last place it should be in a place like this.

"Where's the rest of the Cleaners?" I ask him.

"Rounding up more Necs. It's pretty bad out there. We've been at it for hours. We got most of the uninfected out this morning. But that wasn't easy with bugger all staff."

"What do you mean? I thought you'd have a massive crew up here. Where are they?"

The man snorts. "Massive crew? Fat chance of that. We don't have the budget for it. Same as you lot down your neck of the woods."

"That's why they called us, Cath," Andrew cuts in. "None of us can cope alone with an outbreak this big. There just isn't the staff for it."

"So why are we bringing them here?" I ask, suddenly aware that the Nec I just dragged in is still by my feet. Andrew sees me flinch and grabs the Nec's arm and pulls him over to the aisle with the others.

"Safest place for them while we wait for another lorry to pick 'em up. Lorries can only store thirty at a time, and we can't exactly spare any Cleaners to take them over to Romkirk. It's just easier to keep them all in one place until we can ship them out."

"So where do you want us to start sweeping?" Andrew asks the man.

"Well, I sent your guys down to Marbleview Street about fifteen minutes ago, so if you two can take The Mount."

"Where's that?" Andrew asks.

"Just right as you come out of the church. It's

near the primary school."

"What about the school kids?" I ask, seeing images of children running for their lives, being hunted by a pack of rotten Necs. "Are they still inside?"

The man shakes his head. "No, they're out. That was our first protocol. But you're gonna have to go door to door. Take your van, and fill the fucker up with as many Necs as it'll hold. And get back here ASAP."

"What about the uninfected?" Andrew asks. "Are we getting them out, too?"

"No. There's no time. God knows when it'll be safe for Control to send a bus in here. Just make sure each house is locked down, and concentrate on taking out the Necs."

"Okay. No worries."

The man points to a large box by the entrance. "Take one of those with you. You're bound to run out."

I walk over to it, pull the cardboard flap open and see that it's filled to the brim with muzzles and cable-ties. "*Bloody hell*, there's a lot in here."

"Well, you're gonna need a shit load," the man replies. "As you can see we ran out of body bags a while ago, so you'll have to make do with what you've got. Just bag up what you can and throw the rest on top."

Andrew lets out a long breath, clearly pissed off, and makes his way towards the entrance. "Fine." He then gestures with his head for me to go with him. "Come on, Cath. Let's get moving."

I pick up the box, my mind struggling to process what I've just witnessed, and what I'm about to do.

But still I find myself leaving the church, behind Andrew, to round up a horde of flesh-hungry Necs.

13

As the name suggests, The Mount is a steep street with a row of terrace houses on each side. It stretches up further than my eyes can register, so I'm guessing that there must be over a hundred in total. *We're gonna need a bigger van.* To the left of the junction is a primary school—the gates have been padlocked and there are no obvious signs of life through the windows. *Thank God.*

Climbing out of the van, gun gripped tightly, helmet on, we make our way to the first house.

"How should we do this?" I ask Andrew. "One side at a time?"

"No. We zigzag. It's easier." He points his gun to the first door. "Okay, Cath, we stay methodical—start with number one. But more importantly, we stay together. Don't make a move unless I say so, or you have no other choice. Agreed?"

"Agreed," I say with haste.

Leading the way, Andrew rings the doorbell. There's no response. He pushes the button again, along with a few hard knocks. Still nothing.

"Maybe they're at work," I suggest. "It's still early."

"Might be." He tries the handle. It's locked. He crouches down, lifts up the letterbox flap, and shouts: "Hello. Is there anybody in? It's Disease Control. We're here to help." He listens out but hears no response. "Check the window, Cath."

Knocking on the window, I push my head close to the glass, but my helmet prevents me from going any nearer. I almost pull the horrid thing off but don't, to avoid a telling off from Andrew. "Can't see any movement. Don't think anyone's home."

"Okay, next house," he says, letting go of the letterbox flap. "There's no one here. And if there is, then they're safe enough."

"What if there're Necs inside?" I ask. "Shouldn't we check?"

"No. The place is clear."

"How can you be sure?"

"Because they'd be beating down that door by now. The doorbell would have driven them out."

"Oh, yeah. Good point."

"Come on," Andrew says, "let's just keep

moving. It'll be dark before we know it."

The next house is the same. Deserted. And the next. I'm beginning to think that everyone is at work, or the Cleaner has asked us to sweep a street that has already been swept.

Andrew slams the side of his fist hard into the door several times before we hear footsteps racing to answer it. A middle-aged woman opens the door, her face a mask of panic. "Who the hell are you?" she says. "You better be the police. I've called them three times."

"Madam, we're not the police," Andrew replies, with conviction in his voice. "This whole area's been quarantined."

"*Oh my God,*" she says, bringing her hand up to her mouth as she gasps. "Why? What's happened?"

"There's been an outbreak of Necro-Morbus in Crandale. So we need to check if your home is secure."

"But what about the police? And what about those people?"

"What people?"

"The people I called the police about. Trying to

break down my back door."

"Is there anyone else in there with you? Husband, kids, friends?"

"No, just me," she replies, shaking her head. "My husband is still at work. And my son is still in college."

"Madam, you need to let my colleague and me inside your house to make sure it's safe. Then we need to deal with your intruders."

"By all means," she replies, stepping to one side to clear our path.

I follow Andrew inside and we sweep the house as fast as possible, making sure that every window is closed and locked. More importantly, we make sure she doesn't have any surprise relatives hiding in any of the rooms.

Luckily she doesn't.

In the kitchen, my eyes go straight for the back door and the dark shadows that fill its glass panels.

"Is the door locked?" Andrew asks the woman.

"Yes," she points to the top of the door. "Dead bolted."

A fitting word.

"How many are out there?" I ask her.

She shrugs her shoulders. "Not sure. Maybe four or five. Hard to tell from here."

I give Andrew a gentle elbow nudge. "How about we check from the upstairs window. We may be able to take them out from up there."

"Good thinking, Cath." He redirects his attention to the woman. "Madam, I'm going to need you to go into one of the upstairs rooms, out of the way. Any room with a good lock. Just in case something happens. Can you do that for us?"

"Yes. Of course," she replies, trepidation in her tone.

The three of us exit the kitchen, Andrew leading the way, the woman in the middle.

Upstairs, the woman locks herself in one of the bedrooms. Andrew tries the door handle to be sure. We make our way into a second bedroom, and take off our helmets, setting them down on a wooden chest of drawers. Over to the window, which looks directly down onto the garden, Andrew pulls the blind slightly to the side. I do the same at the other end. Peering down I see four—no *five* Necs, bunched up outside the back door. From here they look pretty fresh, most likely infected a matter of hours ago—which makes doing this job all the more difficult. It's easy not to think of them as human when they're looking like rotten monsters. But these?

Poor bastards.

Taking a closer look, I see that the group is made up of an elderly woman, three middle-aged men, and one teenage girl. The elderly woman's throat has been torn out; dried blood splattered all down her beige blouse and blue cardigan. I can't quite see where the three men were bitten, but the teenage girl's injuries are obvious; her left arm is missing from the elbow down, fresh blood still dripping from the wound. *Christ*, maybe one of those men is her father. *And* the culprit.

I feel sick to my stomach just thinking about it.

"Can you climb up on that?" Andrew asks, pointing down at the thin, plastic windowsill, barely wide enough to hold even *my* foot. "I'm too heavy. I'll break it."

"I'll give it a go."

Using the wall for support, I step up onto the windowsill. I slowly and quietly open the small window at the top of the glass, and then push my head through the gap.

I can hear the moans of the five Necs below.

"Do you think you can get a good shot from there?" Andrew asks.

"Yeah. I should do, just about."

Pulling my gun out of the holster, I bring it up high and squeeze my arm through. Thoughts of dropping it down to the garden fill my head. Even though I can't properly line up the sight, I still try to aim the gun as best I can. I fire off the first shot; it hits a man's skull. Thank God the tranqs come out silent. Only the sound of the Nec falling onto the paving prompts any reaction, just a few additional moans. I fire another, this time hitting the elderly woman in the temple. Then the two other men. For some reason, I leave the teenage girl until last. *God knows why.* What difference does it make? Something inside tells me to spare her—if only for a few seconds.

Andrew takes hold of my hand and helps me

back down onto the carpet. "Nice work, Cath," he says, with a big smile on his face. "Great shooting."

"Glad my measly frame could come in use."

"Exactly. A fat bastard like me would've never got a clean shot through that tiny gap. Not in a million years. None of the guys for that matter."

"Thanks, Andrew."

"Don't mention it."

Helmets on, we walk back down into the kitchen. Time for the clean up.

Even though all five Necs are sedated, Andrew still opens the back door with caution, gun pointed out in front, ready to take out any hidden Necs. Outside, there's a small mass of bodies, laid out on the paving and well-kept lawn.

Surprisingly, I somehow managed to strap the muzzle on the elderly woman and one of the men without flinching too much. It's getting easier. But Andrew securing the teenage girl definitely helped.

We haul the bagged-up bodies through the house and into the back of the van. Andrew makes sure that the house stays locked down, and the woman remains inside.

On to the next house.

We lock down the next six houses. No Necs, apart from three roamers coming up from Richmond. Andrew takes care of them, and we load them into the van.

The street lamps come on in unison as the winter sun starts to set, leaving the sky an orangey brown. It fills me with such dread, such uneasiness, because the night is just around the corner, and the darkness will only make matters worse.

By the forty-seventh house, the van is getting pretty full, with everything from street and garden roamers, to family members bitten, turned and lost in their own living rooms. Such a vile, disturbing thing to witness, to be a part of. I know it's an important, worthwhile job, but it still doesn't make it any easier. As we climb The Mount, house by house, I forcefully put myself into a numb, protective state. It's an easier task standing behind Andrew—let him take the full extent of mental torture. Let him be the bars of the cage that shield me from the horror. He's been here a million times before.

Andrew drives the van a little further up the street; the engine straining from the weight of bodies. Can't see us filling it much more. There's got to be at least thirty detained Necs stacked up in the back, with only about half in body bags.

"Another four houses," Andrew says, stopping the van, "and we'll head back to the church to drop 'em off." He slips his helmet back on. "With a bit of luck the lorry's already turned up, cleared some of those Necs. Hate to see so many in one place. Looks unprofessional if you ask me—especially without bloody body bags. Typical Bristol-lot; can't keep their Necs in order."

"Where the hell is our backup?" I ask. "Shouldn't the bus be here by now? Help clear these people out?"

Andrew climbs out of the van. "I don't know, Cath. It may not be 'til morning, or at least when we clear the church. There's just too many of them. It's still too dangerous for them to get in."

I shake my head in disbelief. "I just hate to think of all those families locked up in their homes, terrified, not knowing when help will arrive."

"Better than being out here," he points out as he knocks the door. No one answers, so we cross the road to try the opposite house. "I hate it as much as you, Cath. And I hate being in such a fucked up situation. I've never seen such a big outbreak since the stadium incident." Just as he's about to pound his fist on the door, he stops.

"What's wrong?" I ask.

"Door's ajar."

My heart beating faster, I follow Andrew into the house, guns at the ready, fully expecting to find the worst. Even though it's nearly dark, the hallway lights are off, which could mean that no one's in, or most likely, whatever happened here happened before sundown. There's just enough light to see, but easier for a pack of Necs to be lurking in the shadows. He switches on the small torch attached to the top of his gun, and a thin beam comes shooting out the front. I do the same, and the light offers just a little more security. Poking his head into the living room, Andrew scans for any Necs. He then stands by the foot of the stairs and pauses for a moment.

"What's wrong?" I whisper.

"Listening for movement upstairs," he whispers back.

I nod, and listen as well. After a few seconds of silence, he leads me back down the hallway towards a door, most likely the kitchen. Just as he's about to open it, we hear footsteps directly above us. My body clenches up as Andrew pushes past me, heading for the stairs. We slink up each creaky step, praying that we don't draw any unwanted interest. At the top, we walk over to the first door. Andrew pushes it with the tip of his gun. It squeaks open, and I see that it's a child's bedroom, most likely a little boy from the posters of *Ninja Turtles* on the light-blue painted walls. Andrew steps inside, kneels down and checks under the bed. I open the wardrobe doors, only to find hanging clothes, scattered toys, and a few boxes.

"Clear," Andrew whispers. "Next room."

"Okay," I quietly reply.

I recoil in fright when I see the man standing in the doorway.

There is a little boy by his side.

I nearly fire my gun as the dread creeps over me,

painting my skin with goosebumps. Andrew puts a hand out to keep me behind him. I gladly take a step back; gun still pointed at their heads.

"Hello," Andrew says, calmly. "We're here to help."

The boy and the man don't respond. I try to make out their faces, but the light is too weak.

"Have you been bitten?" he asks; this time his voice is a little firmer.

Still no response.

"Is there anyone else in the house?"

Still nothing.

Not a good sign.

"Can't we just shoot them in case?" I whisper to Andrew. "In the arm. It's only a tranq."

"Yeah, we can. But not the kid."

"Why not?"

"Tranqs are too strong. It might kill him."

Andrew fires his weapon, hitting the man in the left shoulder.

The man stays on his feet.

He then lets out a deep, guttural moan, and then drops facedown on the floor when Andrew unloads a tranq into his skull.

Suddenly the little boy bolts towards us, mouth wide, howling like a banshee, arms outstretched. Once he's in the bedroom, I see his dismal eyes, his grey skin tone, the bite mark on his forearm. Without another thought, I shoot him between the eyes. From sheer momentum, the boy's sedated body lunges towards me, knocking me backwards onto the bed.

Andrew heaves him quickly off me and throws him down on the floor with a loud thud.

"Are you okay?" Andrew asks, pulling me up onto my feet.

At first I think I am, but when I see the little boy, wearing just a blue T-shirt and a pair of *Ninja Turtle* pyjamas bottoms, his face buried into the carpet, I suddenly feel lightheaded, unsteady on my feet. I retreat to the bed, struggling to catch my breath.

"Take a sec, Cath" Andrew offers. "Have a little breather."

"He was so young."

"I know. But that's the job, I'm afraid."

"He was just a *bloody kid*," I say, my words turning into a sob, "*it's not right.*"

Andrew sits next to me, his arm over my shoulder. He removes my helmet and drops it on the bed behind me. He does the same for his own. "I hate these fucking things," he says, clearly attempting the impossible task of lightening the mood. "They're ugly, hot, and I can't see fuck all."

"*It shouldn't have happened to him,*" I weep, my words barely audible. "*Not to a child.*"

"I know," he replies, shushing me like a baby. "It's horrible sometimes. Especially when there's kids involved. But you know what? The way I look at it, for every kid we have to take out, we may save five in its place. Now I'm no maths expert, but I say that ratio sounds pretty good to me."

I know he's right. I know it's the job, but it doesn't make it any easier. Especially when all I want to do is go home. But I can't. Not yet. I'm all the backup Andrew has. I could never abandon him. No matter how petrified, how low I get.

Sniffing loudly, I manage a thin smile. Not from happiness, or politeness, but of acceptance. I've got a job to do. These people need our help. I've gotta dig deep and suck it up.

This is a warzone, and I'm a soldier on the frontline.

"Let me tell you something, Cath," Andrew says. "Something I've never told any of the guys before."

"What's that?"

"Dead people—*they scare the living shit out of me.*"

I let out a short chuckle.

"It's not funny, Cath," he says, playfully. "Yeah, after a few years they get a little more bearable. But I still hate the sight of them. They still freak me out. And *fuck me* do they give me nightmares. Even now."

"Really?"

"Damn right they do. I can't tell you how many times I've woken up in a cold sweat."

"Well, that's not exactly making me feel any better. I thought it was supposed to get easier."

"Yeah, it does. In time. But my point is, it's normal to be afraid."

"Who says I'm afraid?"

Andrew snorts. "*Cath*, even with the visor on I can see how frightened you are."

I shake my head. "That obvious is it?"

"Yeah, but only to me. Because I know how you're feeling. But you wouldn't be human if you didn't get scared—if you didn't get upset shooting down a kid." He nudges me. "And I only like working with humans."

I return a nudge. "Thanks, Andrew. You're a good guy."

"I know," he gets up off the bed. "Just don't tell the guys for fuck's sake. *Or* my ex-wife for that matter."

Getting up, I unclip a muzzle and cable-ties from my belt. "Let's get these two in the van, and get the hell back to that church."

"Sounds like a plan. If you want, I'll secure the little boy."

"No, it's all right," I say, shaking my head. "I'll do it."

"Are you sure? I don't mind."

"No, I need to get past this. I'll be fine."

Andrew smiles. "Good girl."

Kneeling down over the boy, I start to turn him around. His eyes are closed, which makes him appear as nothing more than a sleeping child. *Peaceful.* Somehow it makes it a little more endurable. I think if his eyes were wide open I'd have to pass. I wrap the muzzle around his mouth and chin, and then buckle up the back. Once I've fastened his wrists together, I move down to his ankles. Just as I do, I hear a low growl coming from the doorway. Turning, I see Andrew on his back, out on the landing, pinned to the carpet by a woman. I leap to my feet, gun in hand and fire three tranqs into the back of her head. The woman goes limp over Andrew's body. Racing over to them, I pull the woman off him.

I gasp in horror when I see the blood pouring out of Andrew's neck.

"Oh my God!" I scream. "What the fuck!" Dropping to my knees next to him, I swiftly place both hands down on the bite, not even sure how much pressure to apply, or even if I'm meant to. But I do it anyway. It's instinct. Andrew tries to speak but his words are a gurgling mess. I shush him, tell him not to speak, tell him that everything will be okay, that we're going to get him to a hospital.

He's not going to die on my watch.

But as the blood begins to seep through the thick fingers of my gloves, pooling under his head, only then does it dawn on me that his helmet is off. Glancing at the bed I see it, next to mine.

Please let him be all right.

Don't let him die.

Don't let him die because of me.

14

My vision blurs from the tears, coursing down my cheeks. Andrew's eyes have started to close. "Stay with me!" *Got to get him out of here. Right now.* I put my gun back in the holster; Andrew's weapon is on the carpet, the torch at the top still on. Pushing his limp body into a seated position, I hook my arms under his armpits. "You're gonna be fine. I promise." I drag his heavy body backwards, inch by inch, towards the stairs, looking over my shoulder for guidance. *Got to get out of this fucking house. Out of Crandale.* I make my way down the stairs, struggling to stay balanced with every step. "You're doing great. Nearly there. I'm gonna get you to a hospital."

My foot misses a step.

I plummet down the last half of the stairs, taking Andrew with me. My body crashes onto the hallway carpet, cracking my head as Andrew's full weight lands on top of me.

Still conscious, I manage to push him off me. Just as I wriggle free, I hear him whisper something. "Say it again, Andrew," I ask him, leaning over to listen.

"*An…tiviral.*"

Shit! The antiviral! I forgot!

I unhook my injection gun, and take out the bottle of clear liquid from the metal case. I clip the antiviral to the top of the gun, and pierce the needle into his neck, opposite his wound. I push the trigger and the bottle empties in an instant.

Please, God, let it work!

Just as I reach for his walkie-talkie to call for back up, the kitchen door flies open, and a flood of Necs come charging at me.

"Oh, shit!"

Standing with my back against the front door, I fire, emptying the tranq magazine in seconds. But there're too many. *Need to reload.* Just before I can get the pack clipped onto the top, they're perched over Andrew's body. I fire another magazine of tranqs into the Necs, but it's too late—his throat has been ripped clean out.

Too late to save him. He's gone.

Have to leave him.

Four more Necs race towards me. One trips

172

over Andrew's body, the others step over him, arms thrust forward, teeth snarling. I swing my empty gun, hitting a dead woman in the face. I do the same to an elderly man. With Andrew's blood still dripping from my gloves, the handle slips out of my grip when I swing the gun for a third time. Leaving the weapon on the floor, I open the front door and rush to the van. With no time even to slam the door behind me, they scramble out of the house, just a few feet away. On the lit up street, I can see another flock of Necs staggering towards me as I wrench the passenger door open and dive inside the van. I slam the door shut, trapping the fingers of a Nec.

Frantically locking each door, I see a swarm of bodies surround the vehicle, clawing at the curved bonnet, beating livid fists against the windows until their hands bleed, smearing congealed blood over the glass.

I'm suffocating!

Need to drive out of here.

I climb over to the driver's side and reach for the ignition—but the keys are missing!

Shit! Where the hell are they? Andrew! He still has

them! I'm fucked! I squeeze the steering wheel tightly as the panic washes over me like boiling acid.

The radio!

Unclipping the receiver from the two-way radio, I bring it to my mouth, push the button on the side and speak.

"Come in, Darren," I say, choking with panic. "This is Catherine Woods. Is there anybody there? Over."

No response. Just static.

"Come in *anybody*. This is Catherine Woods. I need help. We have a Cleaner down. Please, someone. Anyone. We need help urgently. Over."

Still nothing.

"*Please. Darren,*" I beg, my body cramping as the noise outside increases. "If you can hear me, I'm halfway up The Mount, still in Crandale. I'm in desperate need of assistance. *Come in. Over.*"

More static.

"Shit!"

Where the fuck has everyone gone?

I quickly change the frequency. "Come in, Control, this is Catherine Woods," I tilt my badge up from my vest to see the details, "ID number 7762. I need urgent assistance. Over."

"*Roger that, Catherine,*" a man's voice replies through the speaker. "*Reading you loud and clear. Over.*"

I gasp in relief, closing my eyes briefly. "Oh thank God. I need help right away. Please. Over."

"*Are you still inside Crandale? Over.*"

"Yes. I'm trapped inside the van, halfway up The Mount, and I'm surrounded by Necs. Andrew Whitt is dead. And I can't get through to the other Cleaners. What the hell is going on? Over."

"*We don't know what's happened, Catherine. We lost communication about an hour ago. So you need to sit tight and wait for help to arrive. Over.*"

"How long will that take? Over."

"*I don't know yet. I'm sorry. For the time being, you'll have to ride it out. Over.*"

"That's bullshit!" I snap, as I watch more and more Necs reach the van, drawn to the loud uproar. "You can't just leave me here to die!"

"*No one is leaving you anywhere. Help is coming, I promise you. But you have to keep calm—and keep your voice down. You'll only draw more of them to you. Over.*"

I stare at the radio, listening to the riot outside. "Over and out," I say in defeat, dropping the receiver and watching it swing wildly above the dashboard.

I can't breathe.

The sight of so many, loose, is too much to process, to stomach, and I can hear the captured Necs squirming in the back of the van. I want to just curl up into a ball and close my eyes tightly, and wait for the morning to come, for the nightmare to be over. I want Dad to tell me that there's nothing to worry about, that monsters aren't real, that they're all in my head. But they *are* real. *Very* real. And they have teeth dripping with disease.

The van is juddering from the bulk of the Necs. I close my eyes and wait for it to all be over. Wait for the Necs to get bored and wander off to find someone else to feed on. Wait for the cavalry to come and rescue me.

Or simply wait to die.

I can't block out the howls, can't shut out the scratching, the thrashing. All I can do is *nothing*.

But then an electric shock of clarity hits.

My mobile phone!

I can call HQ. Maybe speak with Roger directly.

I pat myself down, hoping to feel its weight in my top pocket. *Shit! It's not here.* Must have left it back at HQ when I changed. *Andrew's phone!* I scan the dashboard, the cubbyhole under the stereo, and the side of the door. I don't see it. Reaching across the gearstick, I open the glove compartment, scooping out its contents over the floor. A map. A tiny screwdriver set. A bottle of alcohol gel. Some tissues. No gun. No helmet. And no bloody phone. Exhaling loudly, I wipe the sweat from my forehead, unable to think of a way out of this hell. *Wish I knew how to hotwire a bloody car.*

These windows won't hold forever. Need to get the hell out of here. Now!

Think, Cath!

I look up, hoping to see a sunroof, but there isn't one. I look behind at the metal separating me from the back. *Maybe I can detach it, and then escape through the back doors.* I push on it hard, but nothing happens. "*Shit!*" At the centre, I notice a small rectangular panel, about twice the size of a cat-flap, with screws at each corner. *I can get through there.* Diving to the floor of the passenger seat, I pick up the screwdriver set. The screws are big so I pluck out the largest screwdriver I find, and it's still about half the size it should be. But it'll have to do. Slowly, I twist out each screw, letting them drop down to the floor. Once each one is out, the panel still doesn't fall off. Removing my blood-soaked gloves, I dig my fingernails into the rim of the panel and start to pull.

It finally pops off!

Looking through the opening, I see the mass of piled up bodies. *Maybe there's even more than thirty.* The bottom layer of bagged-up Necs has been completely buried by the others. The tranqs have already started to wear off on a few. I watch in repugnance as they try to wriggle free from their restraints, their cries stifled by the muzzles. The sound of growls increases, and the van shudders even more from angry fists pounding at the doors and windows. Taking a few deep breaths, I scurry through the opening like a rabbit. Straightaway, I drop down onto a Nec. Luckily this one is still sedated. Crawling over another, then another, my knee digs into the cheek of an elderly lady. She's fully awake; eyes wide with ravenous hunger. Need to keep moving. Don't look at them. *They can't hurt me.*

Suddenly, I hear the sound of a cable-tie snapping. "Oh, shit!" *Got to move now!* Reaching the door, I clasp the handle. *This is it, Cath. You can do this. Come on!* I take another deep breath.

One... Two...

Three!

I shove the door wide open. It slams into a Nec, launching him backwards onto the road. Without a second thought, I'm out of the van and running as fast as I can down the street, heading for the church. I don't turn back, not for anything, not for anyone. Not even when I hear a horde of Necs chasing behind. Have to keep moving. Don't stop.

Ahead, I see the school. As I pass the fence, heart thrashing against my chest, another two Necs spot me and join the pursuit. Don't think I've run so fast in my life. My knee is throbbing, but it's the least of my worries. I see the church in the distance.

Can't see any other Cleaner vans. At the gate, I scramble through, smacking my hip painfully on the frame as I enter the graveyard. Just as I'm about to sprint up the path, I see four Necs kneeling over a Cleaner's motionless body. His helmet off, his throat spewing blood. Torn flesh is hanging from the mouth of a Nec, blood dripping from its teeth.

Oh, shit! We've lost control!

Before the Necs are able to spot me, I turn and scurry back through the gate. Once I step onto Richmond again, the herd of Necs is just behind me. Tearing down the hill, I head towards Rose Avenue and the barricade. Momentum forces me to slam my chest into the side of a parked car—knocking me backwards—but I somehow manage to stay on my feet. The car alarm starts to wail, front lights flashing, drawing attention to another group of Necs coming out of a house on Rose Avenue. I backtrack slightly down a pitch-black lane.

Exhaustion and the pain in my knee are slowing me down. Need to hide somewhere, let them pass me. Barging one of the lane doors open with my shoulder, I scamper into a garden. As I'm about to slam the door behind me, the garden light-sensor comes on, and I'm met by another Nec—a man—ambling on the lawn. He spots me and sprints towards me. I run to the neighbouring wall, but it's too high to scale. Leaping up onto a plant pot, I'm able to reach the top of the wall, but then the Nec catches hold of my vest, dragging me backwards. Losing my footing, I crash-land on the Nec, its jaws clamping down on the thick fabric of my suit. I try to wriggle and twist free, but he's too strong—too fresh. *Too famished.* Driving my elbow into his ribs does nothing. All I can do is squirm.

I'm tempted to scream for help. But I can't. The garden door is hanging wide open. Can't let the other Necs know I'm in here. With every ounce of strength I can gather, I manage to free myself from his jaws and roll away. My kneecap grinds as I get to my feet, heading towards the wall again. Leaping back up onto the plant pot, my knee gives way, and I slam my head against the wall.

Suddenly I'm lying on my back, looking up at the stars of the cold night sky.

My vision starts to cloud.

Can't keep my eyes open.

Have to get up.

Need to get…

The pain in my knee fades to nothing.

The throb in my head vanishes.

All I feel is the weight of something crawling, slithering over me.

And the starry night sky is replaced by the eyes of a dead man.

15

"Can you hear me? You need to get up. I think she's dead…"

* * *

My head is a spinning mess of thoughts. Can't focus on anything for more than a moment. I try to force my eyes open, but it gives me a headache. I can smell something. The scent of nostalgia.

It's freshly-cut grass.

Feels so…familiar, like the first day of spring, or camping out with friends.

Where the hell am I?

"You have to wake up!" Andrew screams. He sounds pissed off with me. Haven't seen him angry yet. What's the problem? Am I late for work? Slept through my alarm clock? Wouldn't be the first time.

"Come on, Josh! You have to get her inside!"

Who the hell is Josh?

Someone from the restaurant perhaps? One of the new guys? Can't recall, but it's tough keeping up with all those new faces. They all start to look the same.

"Are you bit?"

Bit? What's that suppose to mean?

What the hell would have bitten me? The neighbours Rottweiler? No, he's dead. They put him down last year.

"Get up!"

Yes, I can hear you. Stop going on at me. I'll be up in a—

My eyes open and I'm in a garden. On the cold ground. It's night time but everything is lit up by a bright light. There's a young girl, thirteen maybe, standing just ahead of me, a spade in her hand. She's got the sharp end pressed down on something.

Where the hell am I?

Someone is trying to drag me by my arms in the opposite direction. Tilting my head back, I look up at a little boy, about nine or ten, blond hair, his face bright red from the strain of my weight.

"Wake up!" the boy shouts.

After the girl has pulled the spade out of the man's throat, she drives it down again, hard, nearly severing the head entirely.

This has to be a nightmare.

"Come on, Amelia!" the little boy sobs. "It's dead! Leave it!"

She brings the spade down for yet another stab at the man's neck, this time cutting the head off completely. "It's not dead, Josh!"

"Yes, it is!"

"No, it's not, Josh! It can't die!"

The disorientation disappears and a sudden shunt of clarity hits me. I know exactly where I am, what I'm doing on the floor.

Scrambling to my feet, my knee gives way under my weight. I cry out in agony. The boy helps me to my feet, clutching my arm tight with his scrawny hands. The girl drops the spade and bolts towards us, shouldering me in the chest, trying to get me through the back door. I fly into the kitchen. As the door slams shut, I catch a glimpse of the Nec clamber back onto its feet, its head still on the path. The girl twists the lock on the back door and pulls down the blind, covering the glass panel.

The young girl and boy steer me through the

185

kitchen. They lower me onto a chair and I sit, heavily, still not completely recovered from the concussion. "Turn the light off," I say, groggily, pointing up at the bulb on the ceiling. "They'll see us." The girl races over to the wall by the back door and switches it off. The room becomes pitch black and silent.

My head cloudy, knee throbbing, I try to listen out for Necs.

Can't hear any. I think we're safe.

Suddenly a dim light comes on, lifting some of the darkness. I see the girl, standing to the left of me. There's a thin beam of light coming from an extractor-fan, which is positioned directly above a large oven. "Is this too bright?" she asks me, her finger still on the button.

I shake my head. "No, it's fine."

She walks over to the cupboard, pulls a glass out, and fills it up with water at the sink. She places the glass on the table in front of me.

"Thank you," I say, noticing for the first time her bushy red hair, her light-blue top and jeans—and the horror in her large, emerald eyes.

"Are you here to help us?" she asks me, leaning against the worktop, the boy huddled up close to her, his head just about reaching her chest.

"What do you mean?" I ask, the haze in my eyes still lingering.

"Well, you're one of those Cleaners, aren't you? You're meant to help us."

I glance down at my mud-stained uniform, and swallow the water down in one gulp. "Yeah. That's right. I'm a Cleaner."

"Have you come to help us?" the little boy asks, still cowering behind the girl.

I pause for a moment, almost forgetting my job, my whole reason for being in this Godforsaken hellhole. "Yeah. Of course I have. I'm Catherine— Cath. You can call me Cath. I'm a Cleaner."

"Where's the rest of you?" the girl asks. "I saw four vans drive past the house this morning."

"We got into some trouble over by the church."

"What kind of trouble?"

"We got ambushed by a large group of Necs. I got separated."

Shit. I shouldn't have said that. They're too

young.

"But there's more of you coming, yeah?" the little boy asks, his tone laced with worry. "They're on their way, right?"

I rub my eyes, noticing that I no longer have my gloves on, or my helmet. It reminds me of Andrew's contorted face, just before they killed him. I want to cry, but I can't. Not here. Not yet. Not in front of the children. Everything seems so surreal and dreamlike. The journey from The Mount to here seems like it was days ago. Can't seem to shake off this fog—being knocked unconscious, hurting my knee.

The Nec crawling over me...

"You saved my life," I say, only now realising it. "Thank you."

"It's nothing. We had to," the girl says. "We couldn't let that monster bite you."

"But you could have been killed."

"I can handle myself."

"I can see that. How old are you?"

"I'm fourteen. And my brother's nine," she replies, pulling him even closer.

"Well, I'm glad you came out when you did."

"That was Josh. He saw you from the window."

I smile at the little boy. "Josh, is it? Thank you. You saved my life."

"It's okay," he says, shyly. "My sister was the one with the spade."

"Where did you find the courage to do something like that?" I ask her.

Amelia shrugs. "Just didn't want that monster hurting anyone else."

"Did he hurt you?"

The siblings shake their heads in unison. "Not us," Josh says, his eyes welling up.

"Who?"

"It bit Michael," Amelia says.

"Who's Michael?"

"He's our foster dad," he says, sniffing, wiping his nose with the sleeve of his red jumper. "And then our foster dad bit our foster mum."

A cold shudder slithers over my skin. "And where are your foster parents now?"

Josh points at the kitchen door. "They're in the living room."

16

The thought of these children, under the same roof as two Necs makes me almost sick to my stomach. This should never have happened. Someone should have got them out this morning. They should be safe and sound, away from this shit-hole, away from all the infection. Not decapitating bloody Necs in their own garden.

"Is the door sealed off?" I ask by the kitchen door, listening out for groans, signs of movement.

"Yeah," Amelia replies, standing next to me, with her brother by her side, holding her hand. "It's locked from the inside."

"A lock?"

"Yeah. Juliet had one put in last summer after Josh broke one of her ornaments."

"It was an accident!" Josh snaps. Amelia shushes him, and he frowns hard at her.

"How is the door locked from the inside?" I ask, frowning in confusion.

"Juliet locked herself in," she replies. "Before she turned."

"Oh, *Jesus*. What happened?"

"None of us saw Michael get bitten," Amelia struggles to say, clearly holding back her tears. "We just heard screaming. I was in my bedroom, and Juliet was getting Josh ready for school. Michael must have seen the man in the garden and went out to him. He couldn't have known about the outbreak. None of us did. We rushed downstairs to see what the noise was. By the time we got to the kitchen, Michael was crawling across the floor, bleeding from the side of his neck. We saw the man in the garden, blood all over his mouth, limping towards the house. Juliet slammed the back door in his face and went to Michael. She told me to grab a tea towel, to keep pressure on his neck. But it was too late—he died."

I look down at the floor, noticing the faint bloodstain still not completely mopped up.

"Me and Juliet dragged his body into the living room. We put him on the couch and then called an ambulance. But when we got through, they said that we'd have to stay in our homes until Disease Control got here."

"Oh, my God," I say, shaking my head, glancing at Josh's distraught face. *Way too young for all this shit.* "That's terrible."

"Juliet sat with him, crying her eyes out. Don't think she believed he was dead. And she was right. I watched his eyes open. Then he just sat up and took a bite out of her arm. That's when we knew exactly what was going on."

"Is that why she locked herself in with him?" I ask. "To protect you from her and Michael?"

Amelia nods. "She told us to stay away from the door, to not let her out for anything. Josh was crying, so we locked ourselves in my bedroom. And that's when we saw you."

I pause for a moment, trying to think of my next plan of action. So far all I've done is get my partner killed, run for my life, and almost get eaten. Can't screw up now. Not with these kids trapped here. "Where's your phone?" I ask, but then I spot it attached to the wall by the window.

"Who are you calling?" Amelia asks, pointing at the phone. "We've tried calling for help."

"I might have more luck." I dial 999 and within

seconds a woman's voice appears on the other end of the line.

"*999. Which emergency service do you require?*"

"Hi. My name is Catherine Woods. I'm a Cleaner for Disease Control. I'm trapped in a place called Crandale. It's under—"

"*Please hold,*" she says, cutting me off.

There's silence for a few seconds until I hear an automated voice: "*Your area is under government quarantine. Please stay in your homes at all times. Make sure all your doors and windows are locked. Ensure that all lights and loud electrical equipment remain switched off. If a person is showing signs of infection, avoid or contain them until help arrives. Do not attempt to confront infected persons. Above all else, please stay calm. Your area is under government quarantine. Please stay in your homes at all times. Make sure all your doors and windows are locked. Ensure that all lights and—*"

Returning the phone back onto its cradle, I try to hide the grave disappointment on my face.

"What did they say?" Josh asks, hopeful.

"They said to sit tight for now. Help is on the way."

"Is there someone else you can call?" Amelia asks. "Maybe the other Cleaners?"

"I've already tried them on the radio. Can't get through."

"Phone your boss then."

"I don't know the number," I reply, shaking my head, pissed off that I didn't memorise it. "It was saved in my mobile. And I don't have it on me."

"How come you don't know it off by heart?" Amelia asks, frowning, suspicion in her tone.

I sigh, ignoring her question, trying to think of another way to get the number. "Where's your computer? I should be able to find it online."

"It's in the living room."

"*Shit.*"

"It doesn't matter," Amelia says. "We don't need anyone. We've got you. You can get us out of Crandale."

"It's not safe out there. You saw it yourself. There's just too many of them. We need to stay put and wait for help."

"What if Juliet and Michael decide to kick the door open? What are we supposed to do then?"

Amelia snaps.

"They won't. As long as we don't make too much noise. Necs respond mainly to sound and movement. They won't bother us."

What the hell do I know? I'm just a worthless trainee.

"Look, if it makes you feel better," I say. "I'll go check on the door. Make sure it's secure."

I grasp the handle of the kitchen door and twist it. Josh leaps forward, pushing my hand away. "Don't," he says, his words filled with dread. "It's too dangerous."

"I'll be quick."

"They'll hear you."

"No, they won't. I'll be quiet. You and your sister just stay in here, and I'll be right back. I promise."

Amelia takes her brother's hand and pulls him into her. "Just let her go. She's a Cleaner. She knows what she's doing."

Do I?

No partner. No helmet. No gun. No backup.

I open the door slowly and step out into the hallway. The light is on. I see the switch on the wall and knock it off. Can't see anything. There's a faint glow coming from the street lamp outside, leaking in through the glass of the front door, but that's it. As my eyes adjust to the low light, I see a door to the left of the front door. It's closed. Must be the living room. Tiptoeing towards it, all I can think about is Andrew, and why he's not here with me, leading the way, keeping me safe. A rush of guilt washes over me when I picture him taking his helmet off to console me.

Why did I have to cry?

Couldn't I have just sucked it up, let it out *after* the job was done? We still hadn't finished sweeping the house. If I had just swallowed the pain a little harder, cried when I got home—on my *own* bloody bed—Andrew would still be alive.

I stop myself from crying when I reach the living room. Leaning in close to the door, I listen out for movement, for faded growls, footsteps. Peering down at the doorknob, I feel the urge to twist it just to make sure that it's definitely locked from the inside. I mean, what if it's not? What if she turned before she got a chance to turn the key?

Can't even contemplate trying the doorknob, can't risk disturbing them. I'm no match for two Necs. Not now. Not without a weapon or helmet. As long as we're quiet, and we stay away from the door, I can't see them being much of a threat. Help won't be that long, surely. Once they get wind of the extent of problems here, they're bound to send in reinforcements. They can't just leave us here. There's got to be some—

There's a loud thud on the door, followed by a low-pitch moan. I almost scream out in fright but somehow manage to rein it in. Backing away, I retreat into the kitchen.

"Is it safe?" Amelia asks.

"I think so," I reply, my voice lacking any real conviction.

"What do you mean *you think so?* Is that lock gonna keep them in or not?"

"I don't know, Amelia. I can't risk twisting the doorknob in case it disturbs them. I mean, you were there when she locked the door. Did you hear her lock it?"

"Yeah. She did," Josh intervenes. "I heard the

clicking noise."

"Me, too."

"Then we should be fine," I say. "If we leave them be, there's no reason to think that they'll try to get out. So let's just go upstairs and lock ourselves in the biggest bedroom. Wait 'til morning. I'm sure this will all be over by then."

Amelia looks at her brother, her eyes brimming with distrust, and then back at me. "You promise?"

"Of course," I reply. "We'll be fine. As long as we stay together."

"What if they get us in our sleep?" Josh asks, frantically.

"Don't be silly," Amelia says. "We won't be sleeping tonight. Not with those things down here."

He nods, the fear in his wide eyes apparent. "Okay, sis. If you say so."

She pulls her brother in close to her, and kisses him on the top of his head. "Don't worry. I'll keep you safe." She looks up at me. "We both will."

I nod and force out an assertive smile. "Nothing's going to happen, buddy. I promise." I give the kitchen a quick scan. "Do you have any weapons? A baseball bat? Cricket bat? Anything to use as a precaution?"

Josh shrugs. "Don't think so. Not very good at sports."

"We did have a spade," Amelia points out, "but I left it outside when I took the man's head off."

"Okay. Doesn't matter." I go over to the cutlery drawer and pick out the largest knife I can find. It's not very sharp, or big, but it's better than nothing. "This'll do. We won't need it, anyway."

"Should we take our shoes off, Cath?" Josh suggests. "We'll be quieter going up the stairs."

"That's a great idea," I say with a smile. "Why didn't *I* think of that?"

He returns a proud beam and sits on the chair, pulling his white trainers off without loosening the laces. Amelia sits on the other chair and does the same with her blue ones. I crouch down, untie my laces, and yank off my thick boots.

"Keep them with you," I say, and then motion with my head for them to follow me out of the kitchen. "Just in case."

Creeping out into the hallway, knife pointed

straight ahead, I lead them warily towards the stairs. I glance back at the kids as we get to the living-room door; Amelia has her brother's hand held tight. We move even slower past the door, one at a time, until we reach the foot of the stairs. Tiptoeing up, I clench when I hear the slightest of creaks. Luckily, there's virtually no sound by the time we arrive at the top. Thank God.

On the landing, I see four doors, and a small window that looks down onto the garden. "Which room?" I whisper.

Amelia points to a door on the left.

"*Wait*," Josh whispers, pulling out of his sister's hand, swiftly disappearing into one of the other rooms on the right.

"What's he doing?" I quietly ask Amelia. But before she can answer, he emerges with a *Spider-Man* soft toy, holding it tight to his chest.

Amelia rolls her eyes and grabs his hand again, pulling him to the room on the left.

As we enter the large bedroom, I nearly switch the light on but stop myself just before.

Josh closes the door. There's a key in the lock,

so I twist it, and then check the handle to make sure the room is secure. It's almost pitch black apart from the street lamps outside the window, trickling through the thin slit of the drawn curtains. I see a small bedside lamp on the right side of the room and then switch it on at its dimmest setting. Sighing loudly in relief, I sit on the double bed. The two children join me.

"Put your shoes back on," I say, placing the knife on the bedside cabinet, and then slipping my feet back into my boots.

"Why?" Josh asks. "I thought we were going to bed."

"Just in case we have to leave in a hurry."

"Okay," he replies, putting his tiny shoes on, his sister doing the same.

"Is this your parents' bedroom?" I ask, eyes examining the room.

"They're not our parents," Amelia corrects me, with a slight bitterness in a tone.

"Sorry. I'm meant your foster parents."

She nods. "Yeah. We're never allowed in here. They have a key for pretty much all the rooms."

"Why's that?"

"They don't trust us."

"Why not?"

"Because they don't know us."

"So how long have you been with this family?"

"About ten months."

"Oh, right. Not that long then."

Amelia shakes her head. "No. We've been in foster care since Josh was a baby. Michael and Juliet were our eighth family."

"Eighth? Really?"

"Yeah. Social services wanted to keep us together. So it's been hard to find a family that wants two kids. We've had to move around a lot. But it's fine. You get used to it."

"I bet you do. So what happened to your parents?"

"Mum died of an overdose just after Josh was born. And Dad? Well…who knows. Haven't seen him in about ten years. Last thing I heard he was living in Scotland with his new family."

"I'm sorry."

Amelia shrugs her shoulders, dropping the ends

of her lips as if it's no big deal. "Doesn't bother us. We don't need him." She turns to her brother, taking his hand. "Do we, Josh? We don't need anyone. We're better off on our own."

"You're right, you have each other. Must be pretty cool having a brother or a sister."

"Don't you have one?" Josh asks.

"No. Just little-old-me. I always wanted one, though. I was always jealous of my school friends. Having someone to talk to, to look out for."

"What about your Mum and Dad?" Amelia asks. "Couldn't you talk to them?"

"Yeah. I suppose. But it's not the same. Like my Dad, for instance: he's always wanted me to go to university, get a normal job. He thought that me wanting to be a Cleaner was a dumb idea, something only men should do. Even as a little girl, all I could think about was being a Cleaner. I thought it would be the coolest job on the planet."

"Isn't it?" Amelia asks. "Shooting zombies all day? Sounds like fun to me."

I shake my head. "It's not. You see some horrible things. Like you've both seen already. And it's dangerous. I lost a friend today."

"What happened?" Josh asks.

"He got bitten."

"Did he turn?" Amelia asks.

I shake my head. "I don't think so. I hope not."

"That's awful," she says, putting her hand over mine. "I'm sorry you lost your friend. What was his name?"

"Andrew. Andrew Whitt," I reply, struggling to stop myself from welling up again. "But you're safe with me. You don't have to worry."

For the first time I see a tiny smile on Amelia lips, softening that hard-ass exterior. "So how long have you been a Cleaner?" she asks.

I pause for a moment, before answering. *Do I tell the truth, that this is only my second day on the job?* No, I can't. It'll scare the hell out of them. Can't have them panicking. Especially the boy. It's too risky.

So I'll lie.

"I've been a Cleaner for about two years."

"So is this the worst outbreak you've had so far?" Josh asks me, leaning over his sister to look at me, his eyes wide with obvious worry.

"No. This is nothing." *More bloody lies.* "We've had a lot worse outbreaks than this. We're just a little understaffed. That's all. Nothing for you to worry about. This will all be sorted by the morning. *You'll* see."

He nods and then lies back on the bed, his head pressed against the white pillow. "What will happen to them?"

"To who?" I ask, frowning in confusion.

"Michael and Juliet. What will happen to them when your friends come to save us?"

I can't help but stutter as I think of a more child-friendly way to say that they'll be sent to a furnace—and cremated to cinders.

"They get burnt, Josh," Amelia answers for me, her tone harsh, straight to the point.

"Really?" he asks with raised eyebrows.

"*Yep*," she continues. "Everyone who's infected gets burnt. The dead can't be killed. It's the only real way to get rid of them."

"What if *I* was bitten? Would they burn me too?"

Amelia nods. "Well...*yeah*. But I won't let that

happen. Nothing bad's gonna happen."

"You promise?"

She leans over her brother and kisses him on the cheek. "I promise." She then crawls beside him, pulling him in close for a hug.

Poor girl. She's probably had to grow up so fast; had to be a mother to him, trying to keep him safe.

Well now it's my job. And I won't let them down.

I smile at the siblings, as they lie there on the bed, almost oblivious to the danger that lurks outside. Maybe I should just be straight with them. Lay my cards on the table. Give them the honest truth—that I'm in *way* over my head—and know *Jack shit* about being a Cleaner.

After a few minutes, I get up and walk up to the window. Pulling open the curtains an inch or two, I peer down onto the street. Seems quiet. Can't see any Necs. Maybe things aren't as bad as I thought. Maybe the other Cleaners have got it under control. Moving over to the other side of the window, something catches my eye. Just down the street a little, I see a front door hanging wide open. A man comes running out. Then a woman. The man trips up on the pavement and crashes down on the road, facedown. The woman staggers towards his motionless body and mounts him. I wince when I see her tear off his ear with her bare teeth. Then another woman comes sprinting up the street, and starts biting into his hand, ripping off most of his fingers in one wrench. I let the curtain go in disgust and return to the edge of the bed.

"Can I put the TV on, Cath?" Josh whispers.

I shake my head. "I'm sorry, buddy. It's too risky."

"I'll keep the sound down. I promise."

"It's not just the sound. They'll see the flickering lights from the window."

"Okay, Cath. But what are we meant to do then?"

"Nothing we can do, other than wait."

"Can't we play a game?"

Amelia shakes her head, rolling her eyes. "Don't be silly, Josh. We can't play a game. We have to be quiet."

"We can play a quiet game," he offers, his young voice crammed with enthusiasm.

"Just try to get some sleep," Amelia suggests. "We can play games when this is all over."

"But it's still early."

"*Tough.*"

"Suppose we *could* play a game," I say, still mulling it over. "Might distract us."

"Yes!" Josh blurts out loudly.

Amelia and I both shush him simultaneously.

He bites down on his lower lip and then mouths the word: *sorry*.

I smile, almost forgetting about the horrors of today; the headless monster in the garden. *Andrew.* "Okay, Josh, what game do you want to play?"

He shrugs his shoulders. "I dunno."

Amelia tuts. "I thought you had a game in mind."

"No. I only know hide and seek, snakes and ladders, and *PlayStation* games."

"You've never played games with your friends?" I ask. "Maybe on a sleepover, or camping?"

"Never had a sleepover. Or stayed in a tent."

"Oh, right. So what kinds of things are you in to?"

"*Spider-Man*, of course," he replies, holding up his *Spider-Man* soft toy, excitement in his voice, in his eyes.

"Well then, you're in luck, because I just so happen to be the world's biggest *Wall-Crawler* fan. And I'm about to kick *both* your butts in a game of superhero facts."

Josh chuckles. "In your *dreams*. There's nothing that I don't know about him. Bring it on!"

"Okay then," I say, "what was the name of Peter Parker's uncle?"

"*Huh*, that's too easy," Josh replies, smugly. "Uncle Ben of course. *My turn! My turn!*"

"Okay," I say, holding my hand out to silence him, "but you need to whisper."

"Sorry, Cath."

"It's all right, buddy. What was your question?"

"What's the name of *The Green Goblin's* son?" Josh asks.

"Too easy," I reply, a big arrogant grin spread across my face. "*Harry Osborne.*"

"Yeah, that was too easy. Your turn, Sis."

Amelia shakes her head. "I don't want to play."

"We can play something else if you want," I suggest. "Something to suit us all."

"No. I don't want to play any games," Amelia replies. "I just want to go to sleep."

"That's fine if you're tired," I say. "We'll try to be quiet."

"I'm not tired."

"Then why go to sleep then?" Josh asks. "It's still early."

Amelia gets off the bed, lifts the quilt and climbs under, lying on her side, facing away from her brother. "I just want morning to come quicker."

"Are you mad with me, sis?"

"No. Of course I'm not," she replies, lifting her head up and turning to look at him.

"Then play a game with us then."

"No. I think it's best if we get some sleep. Wait for the real help to get here."

"But Cath *is* the real help. She's come here to save us."

"No, she hasn't. She almost got killed outside, and she doesn't even have a gun."

"Look, Amelia," I say, tempted to tell her that

she's completely right, that I'm not the real help. "We don't need a gun. As long as we all stay together and stay locked up in the house, nothing bad will happen. Help *is* coming. We just need to be a little patient. But you're right; maybe you should get some sleep. Both of you. "

"What about you?" Josh asks.

"I need to stay awake. Keep you safe. It's my job."

He smiles. "Okay, Cath. Thanks."

"Don't mention it, buddy."

"What if we need to use the toilet," Josh asks, "in the middle of the night?"

"I'll take you," I offer. "But we need to keep that door locked at all costs. Just in case."

"Okay, Cath."

"Do you need to go right now?"

Josh shakes his head. "No, I'm fine. Just wanted to check."

"Okay, buddy. Try to get some sleep now."

He nods and smiles. "Goodnight."

I return a smile. "Goodnight, little man."

He climbs under the quilt, snuggles up to his

sister, and then closes his eyes. I crawl up the bed next to him, prop up a pillow against the headboard, and sit back. Even though I feel emotionally drained of all life, all energy, sleep seems impossible at the moment. It's too early and I have too many thoughts racing through my head. Wish I had a good novel to occupy my mind. Something funny. Without bloodshed. Without death. Anything to take me away from here; away from the isolation, the horror, the guilt of losing Andrew.

Can't believe he's gone. Didn't even get a chance to get to know him, have a drink with him. But with everything I went through, all the emotional stress, the training, the farmhouse, somehow it feels like I've known the guy for years. He looked out for, stuck up for me.

The only one who did.

I look down at Josh, next to his sister, still clutching *Spider-man*. Never seen siblings behave like these two—so close, so in love. Normally brothers and sisters are at each other's throats, bickering, complaining about eating habits, sharing things. I'd love a little brother or sister. Someone to look out for, to pass down little nuggets of life lessons, tips, things to avoid.

Necs being top on the list.

17

I glance at my watch. 8:34 p.m.

I'm bursting for a pee. Didn't think it would be something to worry about. But it is, and it's very annoying. I should have gone before I locked the door. We all should have. I scan the bedroom, looking for something to pee in. Can't see anything obvious, like a large bowl or a bucket. *I'm not squatting over a bloody bucket.* Not just yet, anyway. I can hold it until morning. It's just mind over matter—mental discipline. My bladder is big enough. It's not going to explode.

I'll just have to avoid thoughts of water, dripping taps, and rainy days. I'll just have to focus on what happens next—what the plan of attack is. I mean, how long is everyone expected to wait until help shows up? A day? Two days? A bloody week? That's not right. And if all the Cleaners have been wiped out, what then? The police? The Army? Cleaners from other parts of the UK? Someone will have to step up. They can't just let everyone fend for themselves. There're too many infected.

This is so screwed up.

I check the bedside cabinet for a telephone. There isn't one. I should have called Mum and Dad when I had the chance, told them that I'm all right, that everything is going to be fine. That I love them more than anything in the world. Even more than becoming a *bloody Cleaner!*

It's probably best that I don't speak to them. No point worrying them. If they found out what had happened, where I was, they'd be at the barricade, Dad in his 4x4, ready to ram the wall. No, best not to think about them. This'll all be over by morning. The kids will be fine; their foster parents will be dealt with and I can go home, back to my family. Back to the real world of nights in, watching TV, and nights out with the girls, enduring drunken guys, slobbering over anything with a pulse. Instead of having to deal with an army of cannibals that don't even *have* a bloody pulse!

I feel so helpless, just lying here, waiting for the coast to clear. Never thought my day would end like this. I had so many high hopes about this job, being out there, making a difference, saving the world from the undead—not holed up in a bedroom, waiting for a big strong man to come and rescue me. *Pathetic.*

Really need a pee.

Can't hold it much longer. Staying awake is going to be hard enough without the added discomfort. *I'll have to go.* Grabbing the knife from the bedside cabinet, I creep off the bed, biting my bottom lip as I try to avoid waking them. That's if they are actually asleep. Haven't heard a peep out of them in a while. The floorboards squeak as the weight of my boots press into the carpet. Wincing, I turn to the kids—no change. Josh is still cuddled up to his sister, and Amelia is still facing the other way. At the door, I twist the key and then slowly pull the handle. The door hinges whine even louder than the floor, but it doesn't disturb them. They both must be so weary, all that stress and adrenaline. *Decapitating that man.*

Poor things.

My heart rate increases when I step out onto the landing. I half-expect the foster parents to be standing in front of me, or that Nec from the garden, his severed head under his arm. Hand shaking with the knife pointed, I slink across the landing and into the bathroom. In the darkness, with the door wide open, I unzip my suit, pull it down to my ankles and sit on the toilet. I close my eyes in relief as my bladder empties. Don't think I could have held out all night. The noise of urine hitting the water in the bowl is too loud. Should have put some paper down to absorb the sound. Too late now, I'm in full-flow. Nearly done anyway. When I'm finished, I have to stop myself, just inches from pressing down on the toilet flush.

If flushing the toilet got me killed, then I'd deserve everything I got.

Back on the landing, outside the bedroom, I push the door open, fighting off the urge to go back downstairs and into the kitchen, just to ring HQ again. Maybe some of the guys made it back to Ammanford, and they're waiting for me to report back.

Yeah, in your dreams, Cath.

When I open the bedroom door and step inside, my grip on the knife tightens in fright when I see

Amelia standing in the darkness.

"*Jesus, Amelia,*" I almost yell, holding a hand over my chest, "you nearly gave me a heart attack."

"Where were you?" she whispers, her tone ice-cold.

I close the door behind me and lock it. "I just needed to use the toilet."

"You left us."

"No, I didn't. I was only gone a minute."

"If you want to go, just go. We don't need your help."

"Don't be silly. I'm not going anywhere. I'm here to help you."

"No, you're not. You never meant to be in our garden. You said yourself you were chased."

"I know that. But I'm only in Crandale to help. This isn't even where I normally work. Bristol needed extra help, so we came. *To help.*"

Amelia sits on the bed, quiet for a moment. But then the silence turns to tears. Quickly putting the knife back in the bedside cabinet, I rush over to her side, arm around her shoulders. "Don't cry," I say, in the most motherly voice I can muster up. It feels

218

unfamiliar to me. "Everything's gonna be all right. You'll see."

She shakes her head. "No, it won't be. It never is."

"Why do you say that?"

"Because nothing ever works out for us."

I pull her closer to me. "Life is sometimes horrible and unfair. But, as long as there is breath in my lungs, I'll keep those monsters away."

"How the hell *can* you? You're just one person—*without a gun.*"

"You're *right*," I reply. "I may have lost my gun, and my partner, but we're gonna get through this by working together. And you and your brother *will* be all right. No matter what. Okay?"

She gives me a subtle nod, and then sniffs loudly.

"You're a strong girl," I continue. "I can tell. You're the same as me. And us girls can survive *anything*—even a sexist job like being a Cleaner."

"Sexist?" she asks, wiping away a tear as it rolls down her cheek. "How come?"

"Because *apparently* this is no job for woman."

219

"Why not?" she asks, dabbing her nose with the sleeve.

"Well, according to the *countless* letters of rejection I got from the government about hiring women, men are just better equipped in dealing with Necs. Women just don't have the strength—physically or mentally."

"But they gave you a job in the end."

"*Yeah*—after I made sure that I was a big enough *pain in the ass* that they'd let me have an interview. And it worked. So the moral of the story is: never take *no* for an answer."

"So what's it like being a Cleaner?"

"To tell you the truth, Amelia, it's hard. At first, I thought it would be the coolest job in the world: shooting monsters for a living. But the reality of it is seeing families ripped apart by this disease, danger all around you."

"So why don't you quit? Why stick it out for two years?"

Should I tell her the truth? Now's a good enough time as any to come clean. No, it's still too dangerous. No good can come of it. Best let her sleep tonight knowing that someone is watching over her. Even if it *is* a trainee. "Because I want to help people. Like you and your brother." I give Amelia a playful nudge to her side. "But maybe I'll quit tomorrow. When this is all over."

Amelia returns the nudge. "Maybe you should. But not before. We still need you here."

Beaming, I stroke her soft, bushy hair. "No worries." I get up from the bed. "Jump back in bed. Keep your brother warm."

"Okay," she replies, getting up and then walking over to the other side of the bed. She climbs under the quilt, drapes her arm over her brother's chest, and closes her eyes. "Goodnight, Cath."

"Goodnight, Amelia," I reply, returning to my previous position; head upright against the pillow, eyes wide open and fixed on the door.

Did I lock it after me?

Paranoia kicks in as I quickly get up and check it. *Locked.* Thank God.

Returning to the bed, I massage my aching knee. Feels a lot better now. It must have popped out and then popped back in. I'm sure it'll be fine. I'll have to start wearing my strap again.

I glance over at Amelia; looks like she's sleeping already. I'm starting to feel a little tired myself. Can't sleep, though. Too risky. Have to fight the urge to close my eyes. No matter how heavy my eyelids get. No matter how drained my body feels.

Have to fight it. For them.

18

I can smell bacon. Mum must be making breakfast. Is it Sunday already? Feels more like a Monday though. Haven't had bacon in months. Forgot how good it smells. Even better than it tastes. Dad must have insisted on bacon, even though the doctor told him to lay off the fatty foods. He says it's the *good* cholesterol that's high with him, not the bad kind. Whatever the hell that means.

I should get up in a minute. I'm sure Mum's been calling me. But it's Sunday. At least let me sleep in a little. It's only fair. That's why God invented Sundays—a day to sleep off hangovers.

Did I go out drinking last night?

Must have. Why else would my head be so fuzzy? Must have been a good night if I can't remember even going out. Those nights are always the best.

I try to pry my stinging eyes open. I can just about make out my bedroom, even though it's still pretty dark in here.

Why is it so dark?

The curtains must be closed.

I can see Mum, hovering around by my bed. Probably trying to wake me. Fat chance with this headache, pounding against my temples. Unless she has a glass of water and two strong painkillers, she's gonna have a fight on her hands.

What the hell is she doing, just wandering around my room? Probably scrutinising the epic mess that's all around her feet.

What happened to that smell of bacon? Doesn't smell as pleasant anymore. Almost rancid, like it's gone off. Don't even think Dad would eat it now. And he'll eat *anything*.

My eyes burn as the room comes into focus. Still exhausted, still not ready to face the day yet. Another hour at least. Why hasn't Mum opened the curtains yet? It's not like her. It's usually the first thing she does, just to wake me by blinding me with sunlight.

But this is not my bedroom.

And that is not my Mother.

My entire body freezes in horror when I see the female Nec stood in front of me.

The dead woman's stare is locked onto the bright streetlight, seeping in through the centre of the curtains; her long black hair soaked through with sweat; her arms slumped lazily against her sides.

Juliet?

Holding my breath, I can hear my heart thrashing against my chest; so loud the Nec must be able to hear. I slowly reach for the knife and grip the handle tightly. Turning my head as if my neck is held in a vice, I see the kids. Both siblings are still fast asleep.

Don't think Juliet has seen us yet. *How the fuck did she get in here?* Did I leave the door unlocked when I went to the bathroom? *No, I double-checked.* Moving my head towards the door, I see that it's hanging wide open. *Impossible.*

Swallowing hard, I prod Josh's arm and then place my hand over his mouth. The moment his eyes open, the second he sees his dead foster mother, I can feel my hand filling with his muted scream. I put my index finger to the centre of my lips to shush him. Eyes wide, he nods, so I remove my hand from his mouth. The Nec wanders aimlessly over to the chest of drawers by the window. Reaching over Josh, I give Amelia's shoulder a prod to wake her, once again managing to catch her scream of horror with my hand when she sees Juliet. I gesture for them to follow me off the bed. Josh shakes his head, his giant eyes filled with tears, his body trembling. Amelia takes his hand and starts to push him towards me. He resists for a moment, but submits when the Nec lets out a low, rasping moan. Taking Josh's hand, I help him from the bed. Amelia crawls across the mattress and quietly steps onto the carpet. The Nec has her back to us, facing the window. I usher the kids out onto the landing, and then pull the key out of the door as I follow them. Just as I'm about to close the door, to trap the Nec inside, Josh suddenly slips past me, and races back inside the bedroom. I stop myself from calling out to him as I watch him reach over the bed and grab his *Spider-Man* toy. The Nec spots him and darts towards the bed, diving across the quilt, snarling. I leap out of the doorway, back into the bedroom. Josh screams when he sees how close his foster mother is. Taking hold of his jumper, I yank him away and drag his tiny body towards the doorway. But it's too late. The Nec lunges off the bed and onto his back. Her weight pulls him onto the carpet, hauling me down with them.

"Leave him alone!" Amelia screams when she sees her foster mother's jaws clamp down on her brother's hand. Scrambling to my feet, I thrust the knife through the Nec's left eye, into her brain, and then drive my leather boot into the Nec's face, forcing her to lose her grip on Josh. Grasping his arm, I wrench him off the floor and out onto the landing. Still with the blade planted firmly in her skull, the Nec storms towards the doorway, so I plunge my heel into her chest, propelling her onto her back. Just before she's up again, I slam the door shut, and frantically put the key into the lock. Her body crashes into the door from inside the bedroom, almost popping out the key as I twist it.

Locked.

Amelia's screams of panic, Josh's painful wailing, the wild roars and fists beating from the bedroom—it's all too much to handle, to take in.

"He's been bitten!" she yells. "He's infected!"

"Shut up, Amelia!" I snap. "You're not helping!"

Josh's sobs increase.

"We have to stop the infection!" she yells. "We have to cut off his hand!"

"*No!*" he weeps. "*You can't cut my hand off!*"

"Enough! You're scaring him."

"What the hell are we supposed to do then?" Amelia demands. "He's been bitten."

"*Please don't cut off my hand,*" Josh yells out, tears and snot running down his face.

"No one's cutting off your hand, buddy," I tell him, taking hold of his arm and inspecting the wound. "It's not that deep. We can use the antiviral shot. Stop the infection before it spreads."

"Yes! The antiviral!" Amelia shouts out. "Where is it?"

I reach into my vest pocket only to find it empty. "Shit!" My stomach turns when I realise that I already used it on Andrew.

"What's wrong?" Amelia asks.

"It's gone."

"What do you mean *it's gone?*"

"I had to give it to my partner."

"Get another one then."

I shake my head, struggling to think straight. "I don't *have* another one."

"Well what the hell are we supposed to do now?"

I don't have an answer.

The sweat is now dripping profusely down my face, stinging my eyes. I wipe it away as I look down at Josh. He has his hand clasped tightly with his other hand, blood seeping between his fingers, his face pale. Suddenly everything seems dreamlike, everything in tunnel vision. The Nec, Amelia's words, the screaming, none of it feels real, like I'm in some horrible nightmare—a nightmare that I can't seem to shake off.

But Amelia screaming the name *Michael* at the top of her voice pulls me back to reality, and I'm faced with the foster Dad, shambling towards us from the top of the stairs.

"Watch out, Josh!" I shout as I push past him, ramming both palms into Michael's chest. The Nec crashes down onto the floor, his head smacking against the banister. Within a split second, I'm standing over the dead man, stamping my boot into his mouth with every ounce of strength I can summon. I watch his nose split, then become nothing more than a dark patch on his face. I watch his mouth fill with blood and broken teeth, his eyes disappear into his skull, his forehead split open, and his brain spill out like vomit.

But he doesn't die.

He can't die.

He's already dead.

But he won't be getting up. He won't be hurting anyone tonight.

Not without a face…

19

"You need to get another one right now!" Amelia screams at me as she runs a cloth under the kitchen tap. "He's infected."

"Shut up, Amelia!" Josh cries from the table, clutching his wounded hand. "I'm not infected! Stop saying that!"

"Look," I say, standing beside Josh, trying to sound as calm as I can, "I'll go outside to the van. It's parked up on The Mount. There'll be spare antiviral bottles in the back. In one of the compartments."

Kneeling down in front of Josh's chair, Amelia gently cleans the gouge with the cloth. "Okay. You need to go now then," she orders me, her words shaky, desperate. "Before it's too late."

I nod, and then wipe the sweat from my forehead. Can't quite believe that I'm actually going back outside—back to that *hell*.

But I have to.

"What if something happens to you?" Josh asks, his eyes filled with apprehension, his face white as a sheet. Not sure if it's from the shock or the infection. *Please God let it be from the shock.* "What if you don't make it back?"

"It won't come to that. I won't let it. I'm fast. Faster than any Nec. I'll get those bottles. And you'll be fine. I promise."

"You better go now," Amelia says, "before it spreads."

"Okay. I'll go out the back door, through the lanes. It's darker. Less chance of being seen."

"What about the man in the garden?" Josh asks. "He's still out there."

"Don't worry," I reassure him. "He can't hurt me."

"You don't have a weapon," Amelia points outs. "You'll be killed."

"The spade's still out there, yeah? I'll use that." I unlock the back door. "Just keep the pressure on the bite and I'll be back in no time."

"You promise?" Josh asks. "You won't leave us?"

I turn to him with eyes of sincerity. "*Never.*"

"Take this with you." Amelia hands me a key.

"It's for the front door. Just in case. But I'll be waiting by the back door to let you in."

I take the key and slip it into my pocket. "Thanks. You're a smart kid."

She gives me a slight nod. "Be careful out there."

"I will. Keep the lights out and keep your eyes on the garden."

Stomach twisted with nerves, I clutch the handle and start to pull.

"Wait!" Josh sobs. "Don't go!"

I release the handle and turn to him. "I've got to, buddy."

"*No.* This is all my fault."

"Don't be silly," Amelia says, a deep scowl of confusion on her brow. "How can any of this be your fault?"

"It was me!" he confesses, snot and tears streaming. "*I* did it! *I* left the bedroom door unlocked! When you were both sleeping...I went out for a pee. I was *bursting.* I must have forgotten to lock it." He sniffs loudly. "I'm sorry, Cath."

"You have nothing to be sorry for," I reassure

233

him. "If your foster parents could break out of the living room, then they could have got into the bedroom. So just forget about it. It wasn't your fault. Okay?"

Amelia kneels beside her brother and pulls him in for a hug. "Just go," she says. "We're running out of time." She kisses the top of his head. "Save my brother."

"I will," I reply, pulling the back door open. "Just stay in the house."

I step out into the darkness of the garden.

I hear the door lock behind me, and the realisation that I'm alone again hits me. The garden is cold and silent. I can't really recall being here; everything that happened seems unreal, like the memory of a faded dream, a *nightmare*. I remember my knee giving way, and then staring up at the stars.

My stomach roils when I remember the face of the Nec, glaring down at me, ready to tear my face clean off.

I see the spade lying on the ground next to a bucket. When I'm within reaching distance of it, I can clearly see that it's *not* a bucket.

It's a head.

I quickly pick up the spade, unable to avoid staring at the Nec's face, still very much conscious, his jaws snapping at fresh air, his eyes wide with a hunger that can never be satisfied.

Not without a body.

Body.

What the hell happened to the body?

No time for curiosity. I've got to get that antiviral—*and fast.*

But what about all those captured Necs in the back?

And the one's from the front of the van? What if they're all still there?

Just suck it up, Cath. What other choice do you have?

I check the time on my watch. It's 11:05 p.m.

Feels much later.

Weapon in hand, I race along the garden, towards the lane entrance. Poking my head out, I check for any wandering Necs. Can't see any, but it's dark. I listen hard, but I only hear a slight, icy breeze in the air. I start to jog up the lane towards the street. I should go slower, plan out every step, but

235

there's just no time to spare. He doesn't stand a chance if I'm not back soon.

What if I'm already too late?

At the end of the lane, I see a sign for Richmond. Street lamps dimly light the road and pavements. I can't see any Necs yet. Maybe it's all over. Maybe the other Cleaners have managed to take back Crandale. It's been long enough.

Body hunched, I make my way along the pavement and then duck down by a parked car. The coast seems clear, so I bolt across the road and crouch behind another car. Still no Necs. *This is promising.* Just up the hill I see the church. Never again will I set foot inside one without imagining all those squirming bodies. I run up the road, directly opposite the church, heading towards The Mount. At the foot of the hill, I slow down to catch my breath. My knee is still sore, and the spade is starting to get heavy.

Just up ahead, I see my Cleaner van, the back door still hanging open. I can't see any roaming Necs. They must have scattered, got tired of waiting. I start to creep towards the van, aware that a horde could come busting out of these houses at any moment. When I'm about twenty metres away, I see a few bodies dangling out, some squirming on the road, others with their torsos half in, half out of the van.

I check out the front of the vehicle. It's clear, so I return to the back doors. Spade at the ready, I can see that each Nec seems to be still restrained—limbs tied, muzzles over mouths. The smell hits me like a cloud of toxic gas, causing me to shield my mouth, nose and watering eyes. I can't quite believe that I'm back here. The last place I thought I'd see again.

Shit! Can't remember which side the antivirals are stored: left compartment or right?

I'm sure it's the left.

Using the spade, I push the dangling Necs off the van, and their limp bodies roll onto the road. I focus on Josh's sweet, innocent face, as I climb up onto the van platform, stepping on the arm of a Nec in the process. As I let go of the spade and swim through the dead bodies, I imagine that it's nothing more than having to fish out a set of car keys from a muddy drain. I'm not crawling through a small army of the living dead. It's just a simple task, something that no one wants to do, but has to do regardless. That's all. Nothing more.

Yeah, keep telling yourself that.

At the left side of the van, I try to reach the compartment, my arm rubbing between metal and a sedated dead woman. Most of her dress is ripped so it's just cold flesh grazing against my hand. The stink is almost too much to stand, so I hold my breath as I work my fingers down. The weight of Necs is too great—I can't seem to reach it. With every ounce of strength in me, I pull the woman's body towards me, and manage to create a little more space. With just enough of a gap, I reach blindly, and I'm able to get the compartment open. It's only about twelve inches deep and about the same in width, so I grab whatever the hell is in there. When I see only a pack of antibacterial wipes and a first-aid kit, I almost scream at the top of my lungs, in frustration, in absolute horror. But I stop myself, take a deep breath, drop the items, and start to move over to the other side of the van.

Just as I reach the right side, I hear a loud hiss

coming from outside. I freeze, playing dead, as if I'm nothing more than a captured Nec, and wait for the sound to disappear. But it doesn't, instead it lingers. I contemplate leaping out, confronting the Nec, slicing its head off with the spade—but I don't. It's not worth it. Don't know how many there are. There could be ten of them—and weapon or not, I wouldn't stand a chance. The number of bodies this side of the van is much higher, with zero room to squeeze a hand down to the compartment, let alone open it. I'll have to drag some bodies out of the van.

How the hell am I supposed to do *that* discreetly?

Please, God, give me a break!

The noise is getting closer, as if it can smell that someone is alive in here. Need to kill it if I have any hope of retrieving the bottles. Slowly working my body along the sea of infected, I lock my eyes on the road, through the gap between the doors. Still can't see the Nec. I can feel my shoulders tighten as the fear starts to swallow me.

Got no time to be scared. The clock is ticking.

Reaching the opening, I grab the spade, take in a

lungful of mouldy air, and leap out onto the road. The van door is blocking my view of the Nec so I quickly step forward to confront it, swinging the weapon blindly in the air.

When I see him— the rotten mess of a man— crawling on the concrete, I'm nearly sick to my stomach. Not because of the missing legs, the lifeless, cold eyes, and the thick trail of blood and gore being dragged along the ground. None of that matters. All I feel is a deep sense of loss, of sadness for this poor man. Andrew was my friend. And to see him like this twists and rips my heart in two. The sight is unbearable. My former mentor reaches up to me, his hand still wearing the company-issued gloves. There's no strength in this Nec, no anger. Just a virus, trying desperately to cling onto its host—a host that barely has enough body to control. When he snarls at me through bloodied teeth, I don't flinch. I don't feel horror.

Instead I burst out into tears, just as I did when I shot the little boy. But this time I don't have Andrew to ease my suffering, to reassure me that everything'll be okay, that this job will get easier.

Instead I'm all alone, stuck in this Godforsaken place, with the lives of two children in my hands.

"I'm sorry, my friend," I sob, pointing the spade at Andrew's half-eaten throat, "but I have no choice." And then I drive the sharp metal through his neck, slicing his head clean off.

Taking in deep, measured breaths, I stop myself from screaming into the night, trying not to look at the severed head rolling down The Mount. Instead, I focus on reaching into Andrew's vest pocket, and removing the antiviral case. I open it and see a bottle of clear liquid.

Undamaged.

A warm feeling of elation fills my stomach, rushing up to my chest, as I slip it into my pocket.

I don't look at Andrew's mutilated body, still very much alive, with hands still trying to grasp my legs. I don't let myself. All I see is a big strong man, smoking his cigarette, smiling at me, rolling his eyes at all those other narrow-minded, dickhead Cleaners. Not this…*thing*.

I'm sorry I couldn't save you today. But you saved us. You've saved Josh. Even in death.

Thank you, my friend.

Running as fast as I can down the hill, I throw thoughts of Andrew's head to the back of my own. I can't let it slow me down, not when I'm so close to saving Josh. At the bottom on the street I see the lane entrance—*it's teeming with Necs!* There's at least eight limping along the pavement as if somehow patrolling my only way in.

"Shit," I mutter to myself as I squat down behind a parked car. I'll have to go 'round to the front of the house instead. Staying low to the concrete, I sneak across the road without them spotting me. From the top house on Marbleview, I peer down at the street. Everything *seems* quiet enough. *Please let it stay that way.* I sprint down, eyes darting back and forth for surprise attacks. Just a few houses away, I hear the sound of glass smashing. I quickly duck down by another car and wait to find out where it came from. Ahead, I see three Necs scrambling through someone's shattered living-room window, unaffected by the dead flesh scraping against the razor-sharp pieces still in the frame.

My heart races even more as another two come charging out, as if they have no further use for whatever was in the house. Their moans are loud, causing another four Necs to stumble out of an open front door just across from me.

There're too many of them. I can't risk them seeing me going into the house; they'll storm the place, draw attention to it, and then there'll be an army of Necs at the door. "Shit. Shit. *Shit!*" I say under my breath. I'll have to wait it out.

But Josh doesn't have *time* to wait!

A minute or so goes by and I watch with dismay as even more Necs join the pack. I count fifteen in total. Too many to take on with the spade. Maybe I should try the lane again—it could be clear by now.

Just as I'm about to retreat up the road, I hear an ear-piercing whistle coming from the bottom of the street. I turn my head and gasp in shock. Standing about thirty metres from the Necs is Amelia.

Where the hell did she come from?

"Come on, you rotten fuckers!" She screams at the top of her voice, gesturing with her hands for them to follow. "Come and get me!"

What the fuck is she doing? Is she nuts?

Without hesitation, the Necs start to charge down the hill toward her, snarling like starved animals. Within seconds, the front door is clear. I race to it, spade in one hand, key in the other. *Please, God, let her be okay.* When I'm safely inside the house, I quickly close the door and lock it, and then race into the kitchen. Josh is sitting at the table, holding up a bandaged hand; the colour drained from his cheeks.

"Did you get it?" he asks, groggily. "Did you get the antiviral?"

"Yes. I got it."

"And did you see Amelia? Is she safe?"

"She'll be fine, Josh. Don't worry."

I sit next to him and pull the bandage up a little to inspect the bite. There's a mixture of dried blood around the teeth marks. The veins in Josh's hand have started to turn black. *Not a good sign.* I roll his sleeve up all the way to his shoulder. Pulling out the injection gun from my vest, I clip the antiviral bottle onto the top. Can't quite believe I'm about to give a nine-year-old boy an injection. What if I miss? Hit a nerve, or an artery or something?

That's the least of my worries!

"Is it gonna hurt?" he asks, looking up at me, his eyes vast with dread.

I shake my head. "Only a little sting. Nothing to worry about. And it'll be over in a second."

He nods his head and closes his eyes tightly.

Trying to keep my quivering hand from shaking, I stick the tiny needle into the flesh of his upper arm, and then push the white trigger. Trying to ignore the sobs coming from Josh's mouth, I focus on the liquid quickly disappearing from the bottle. I carefully pull out the needle and put the gun on the table. "Well done, buddy. All over."

Josh opens his eyes, wipes the tears away and sniffs hard. "That hurt a lot, Cath."

"I'm sorry. But it's finished now."

"Will you still have to cut my hand off?"

"No, of course not. We'll just have to wait a little to see if it's worked."

"But what if it doesn't?"

"Then we'll cross that bridge when we come to

it. All right?"

"Okay."

"Good boy."

Getting up off the chair, I make my way over to the sink and pour two glasses of water. Still exhausted, I swallow it in one, and then return to the table and give Josh the other. He takes a sip and starts to unroll his sleeve.

"How are you feeling, buddy?" I ask, placing my palm over his forehead to feel for a temperature. "Any fever?"

"No."

"Well, you're not burning up, so that's a good sign.

"When's Amelia coming back?"

"I'm sure she won't be long," I reply, trying desperately to conceal the worry I feel swirling around my stomach. "She'll be fine."

Will she? I don't know. Maybe. She's pretty strong. And clever. Plus, she probably knows these streets better than most.

"She told me to keep an eye out for you in the kitchen," he continues, "while she looked from my bedroom window."

"What, she went upstairs on her own? After what happened earlier?"

He nods.

"*Bloody hell*, your sister's something else."

"She's not scared of anything."

"I don't doubt it. She's pretty brave. Much braver than me."

"And me."

"Oh, I don't know about that. You've been through a lot tonight, too. How's your hand?"

"It stings. But it's not that bad. It's not as bad as when I sprained my wrist."

"Oh, that sounds painful," I say, eyes fixed on the blackened veins, waiting, *praying* for them to disappear. "How did you manage that then?"

"I fell."

"Really. From where?"

"At school. One of the boys from my class pushed me down the stairs by the corridor."

"That's awful. Why did he do that?"

"Because he's a bully—and bullies don't like foster kids. They used to call me a scrubber and they'd kick me under the table at lunchtime. They're horrible."

"So what happened to the bully? Did you tell the teacher?"

"No. I couldn't. He said he'd kill my sister if I told my teacher or my foster parents. And then I'd have nobody left to look after me."

"He sounds like a rotten little boy. So what happened then?"

"Nothing. He said sorry to me a few days later."

"Really! How come?"

"Well, he didn't say anything about not telling Amelia. So she went down to where he lives, which is not that far from here, and punched him in the nose. She told him that if he ever touched me again she'd kill *his* parents instead. And then he'd be a foster kid, too."

I can't help but laugh. Even with everything that's going on. "Well, as much as I don't condone violence," I lean into him and whisper, "it sounds like the little *shit* deserved it."

"Definitely."

20

Josh has been sleeping for the past fifteen minutes. I wish I could take him up to his bed, but Michael's twitching remains are still up there. Instead, I've pushed two kitchen chairs together, and thrown a coat over him to keep him warm.

Why is he sleeping?

Hard to tell if it's the antiviral taking effect.

Or the virus.

I pray it's the former as I watch the back door for Amelia to return. It's already been too long. Where the hell is she? I feel the need to look for her but can't possibly leave Josh alone.

Shouldn't have left Michael up there on the landing. Maybe I'll drag what's left of him into one of the other rooms. Josh'll be okay on his own for a few minutes.

I put my palm softly on his forehead; there's no fever. That's something at least.

"Amelia?" Josh croakily asks, his eyes half-open.

"Try to sleep," I whisper. "She'll be home soon enough. I'm sure of it."

"Why hasn't she come back yet?"

"She's probably waiting for the right moment."

"Why?"

I shush him like a baby, stroking the top of his head. "Try not to worry; she's a clever girl."

He closes his eyes. I watch him for a minute or two until I'm certain he's fallen back to sleep. Quietly getting up off my chair, I make my way out of the kitchen and into the hallway. As I pass the living room door, I glance inside at the empty room, once host to their foster parents. I notice the lock; it's broken completely off, taking with it some of the doorframe. Visions of Juliet in the bedroom, biting Josh's hand, flood my mind. I see myself sticking the knife into her eye; it sends a cold quiver of repulse through me.

What's to stop her breaking out again?

She's clearly more than capable.

No, she isn't. She probably had Michael's help the first time. There's no way she could have done that on her own.

Could she?

I climb the stairs and reach the landing. My

heart shudders when I see Michael's remains, still convulsing, nails scratching at the carpet. I try not to look at his face—*what's left of it*. It's too much, even after everything that's happened today. Without a second thought, I pull out two cable-ties from my vest, and secure his limbs. I don't bother with the muzzle; he no longer has a mouth. I drag his moving corpse into Amelia's bedroom. There are *worse* places to leave a Nec—but not many.

I close the door and return to the landing.

"*Shit*," I mutter when I hear the back door slamming shut. "Josh! Wait! Don't go out there!"

I race down the stairs, towards the kitchen, my stomach churning at the thought of him outside alone—injured.

Sick.

Turned?

"Josh!" I shout as I burst into the kitchen.

"She's home!" Josh says, hugging his sister tightly as she catches her breath. "She made it! She's safe!"

I gasp with relief.

Just to see her face again, in one piece, makes

me almost want to cry my heart out. But I don't, instead I go to her, take her by the hand and bring it up to my chest. "Thank God you're safe."

Still struggling to breathe, Amelia sits down at the table.

I quickly fill up a glass of water and hand it to her. "I don't know if you're crazy, stupid, or brave—but what you did out there was beyond belief."

"Thanks," she manages to say between gulps of water.

"That's not a compliment," I reply, shaking my head. "You could've been killed. What the hell were you thinking? You're just a kid."

"This *kid* was busy trying to save my brother's life. *And yours.* If I hadn't distracted those Necs, you would have never got back in one piece."

"But what if they'd caught you?"

"But they didn't. They were pretty slow. Most of them anyway."

I go quiet for a moment, unable to think of anything worthwhile to add.

"Look," Amelia continues. "I don't care about

how stupid I was; all I care about is my brother." She reaches over and takes hold of Josh's wounded hand. "Did you get the antiviral?" She peels back the bandage.

"Careful, Amelia," Josh says, pulling his hand away. "It still hurts."

"We need to see it," I tell him. "Otherwise we won't know if the medicine worked."

Josh slowly begins to unravel the blood-soaked bandage, revealing the bite mark.

"Is it better?" Josh asks, a slight whimper in his voice. "Am I gonna turn into one of those things outside?"

A huge smile of relief covers my face when I see that the blackened veins have vanished. "I think you're going to be fine," I reply. "You haven't been sick, and you don't have a fever. It looks like it worked."

Amelia grabs his arm, pulling his hand up to her face. "Let me see." Instead of smiling, she lets out a drawn-out groan. "Oh thank God," she says, pulling him in for a hug. "Don't scare me like that again. Okay?"

"Okay, sis. I promise."

I watch them for a moment, letting their love for each other take me away from this nightmare. I almost want to cry.

But I've cried enough today.

I pull up a chair next to her. "So what happened out there? You were gone for so long. Josh has been worried sick. We both were."

"Well," she takes another sip of water, "after they chased me down the street, I hid behind a car, and then when they'd passed me, I made my way back up the lane. But the middle of the lane was packed with Necs, ten, maybe fifteen, so I had to wait in one of the gardens. I stayed in a shed until the coast was clear."

"That sounds pretty horrible," Josh says. "So they didn't bite you then?"

Amelia snorts. "What, me? As if. They'd have to catch me first."

"Jesus Christ," I say. "And I thought *I* was a hard ass."

"Foster kids have to be tough. Isn't that right, bro? We don't take crap from anyone."

Josh nods proudly.

"So are you sure you managed to give those Necs the slip?" I ask.

"Yeah. Of course. They were easy. Dumb as cows. I just climbed over—"

Suddenly the glass panel of the back door shatters, spraying shards all over the kitchen floor.

"Oh, shit!" I scream as I watch a pack of Necs scramble through the opening, foaming dripping from their ravenous jaws.

"*Ruuuuuuuun!*"

21

The house is alive with growls of the dead.

Inside the hallway, I barge open the kitchen door and hold it shut, the weight of multiple Necs scratching and pushing behind it.

"What are we going to do?" Amelia screams; Josh is holding onto her arm, tears streaming down his cheeks. "There's too many of them!"

"We need to get out of this house," I say, with no time to weigh up a real plan. "Open the front door, Amelia."

Eyes wide with terror, she slowly pulls it open, but then is jolted backwards, taking her brother with her, as a dead-man tries to enter the house. I have no choice but to let go of the kitchen door and race over to help. I push the front door shut, trapping the Nec half inside. "Get upstairs!" I scream. "Now!"

The hallway starts to fill with a small army of Necs from the kitchen. I release the front door and then bolt up the stairs.

On the landing, I see Amelia holding a long

wooden stick with a hook on the end, trying to reach the attic hatch on the ceiling. "Leave it!" I shout. "There's no time!"

"No! It's the safest place! Just keep them back!"

With no time to argue, I start to kick out at the Necs climbing the stairs, using the banister and opposite wall for support. "Hurry up!"

"Nearly got it."

One of my kicks misses a female's face, so I grab both her wrists and push her hard. She plummets down the stairs, taking three other rotters with her. I hear the sound of the attic hatch opening. Turning, I see a thin metal ladder materialise on the landing.

"Come on, Cath!" Amelia calls out as they race up into the ceiling. I follow closely behind. Halfway up, I feel the grip of a Nec on my ankle. I kick out wildly, managing to free my leg. But more and more are coming up the staircase, filling the landing. I race into the darkness of the attic and try to pull up the ladder, but the heft of bodies from below is too much.

"Pull it up!" Amelia shouts from behind me.

"I can't!" I reply as I drive a boot into a female Nec as she tries to climb. "There's too many of them!"

"Throw something at them!" Josh yells.

Reaching blindly to my side, I feel a large box. It's heavy, so I drag it along the floor until it drops down the ladder, hitting the Nec in the face, splitting her nose like a piece of wood. Amelia slides a second box towards me, and I push it off. It slams into the chest of a Nec, propelling him off the ladder and into another rotter. With the ladder clear of bodies, I start to retract it fast. I struggle past the clutches from reaching Necs, but only for a moment. And then the groans become muffled sounds when the ladder is up, and the hatch clicks shut.

And then complete and utter darkness.

Body trembling, still in a state of shock, I breathe heavily through my nostrils, waiting, *praying* for some great escape plan to suddenly appear.

"Where's the light switch?" I hear Josh whisper.

"I don't know," Amelia answers. "There should be a pull-string somewhere."

I reach about in the blackness until I feel a thin string hanging just in front of me. I pull it and the attic lights up. I scan my surroundings quickly, looking to see if the floor is safe to walk on. It's not. There are various sized boxes, filled with board games, toys, Christmas decorations, and other neglected junk, some rolled-up insulation wool, and a wedding dress, hanging from a ceiling hook, covered in a thin, protective plastic. "Stay on the wooden beams, kids," I whisper. "Or you'll fall through the floor. It's not safe up here."

Josh nods as he puts his legs completely onto a thick beam. "What do we do now?"

"We wait," I tell him.

"For what?"

"For help to come."

Amelia crawls along the beam to her brother. "There's no help coming. It's just us—and them."

"Stop it, Amelia," I whisper loudly. "Help *is* coming. We just have to be patient. Those Necs will leave when they're hungry enough."

"But they know we're up here," Josh says. "They'll wait for us."

"They'll soon forget," I reply. "As long as we stay quiet."

"You promise?"

"I promise, buddy. We'll be all right up here. Safest place in the house. Your sister saved us again."

"I didn't save anyone," Amelia says, coldly, her eyes down on her brother's injured hand. "I brought them here, to the house. They followed me."

"Don't be silly," I reply. "None of this is anyone's fault. We're all just stuck in the middle of a nightmare, and we need each other to get through it. So I don't want to hear about any blaming. Okay?"

She doesn't answer.

"Okay?" I repeat—firmer this time—but still whispering.

After a few seconds, she looks up at me and nods. "Okay."

"*Good*. Now let's just stay together and we'll be all right."

"Amelia, you left the hook on the landing," Josh points out, his tone filled with worry. "What if they use it to get the ladder down?"

"Don't worry, bro," she replies. "They may be fast, but they ain't smart. Well, not *that* smart."

Josh nods, grasping his sister's arm tightly, the fear engraved in his eyes—eyes that have seen way too much horror for a lifetime, let alone a day.

There is a small hole by the hatch. I peer through it and look down onto the landing. The entire floor and stairs are teeming with the dead, some just wandering around aimlessly, while others stare up at the hatch with confused, bitter expressions. And it's only going to get worse with the front and back doors exposed. There's no way we're getting out of here anytime soon. We'll have to just sleep up here, for days if that's what it takes. Hopefully it won't get too cold.

I look around the attic for something soft for us to lie on. *Maybe an old sleeping bag, or a sack of clothes.* I stand up on the beam, holding onto the roof for balance, and then make my way over to the largest box I can see.

"Where are you going?" Josh asks.

"I'm just looking for something to sit on. These wooden beams are uncomfortable. We may be up here a while."

"Why don't you use the wedding dress?" he suggests, pointing over to it.

"Good idea, Josh."

"Can I help?"

"No, it's all right, buddy. Just stay close to your sister. We can't have too much movement up here; it might agitate them."

"Okay, Cath."

Reaching the dress, I tear off the dusty, plastic cover and stare at the stunning white gown for a moment, unable to see anyone other than the infected-version of Juliet wearing it. Should I leave it here? Out of respect?

Don't be so stupid.

She's dead. She doesn't need it. Her foster kids are more important.

I unhook the dress and drag it over to him. I lay it over a beam. "Here, Josh. It's not ideal but it's better than nothing."

"Thanks, Cath," he says as he climbs onto it. "It's comfortable."

"*Great*," I reply. "I'll find you something too,

Amelia."

"Don't worry about me," she says. "I don't need anything. I'll be fine."

"But we don't know how long we'll be up here. It might get cold."

"I'll be all right. Don't fret."

She's a stubborn little girl—I'll give her that. "Okay, but if it gets cold—"

"Then I'll tell you."

I hate being up here. I know it's the only place they can't get to, but I just feel so trapped. I despise the thought of not having an escape route. I mean, what if they never stop coming? What if they quarantine the whole of Crandale—permanently? What then? We'll starve to death. No, we'll die of thirst before that. We'll be able to go without food for months. Or is it weeks? And what about Josh? How long will *he* last without food or water? I can't bear the idea of him withering away in front of me. And what about Amelia? Despite everything she's capable of, everything she's been through, she's still just a kid.

Oh God, please let them be all right. Don't let them die

up here.

Shut up, Cath!

They won't die! Not with me watching over them. Experience or not, I've kept them safe this far—so I'll be *damned* if I'm gonna fail now.

Palms behind my head, I lie back on the beam. It's wide enough to balance my weight, and it doesn't hurt. At least not at the moment. I'm sure it'll hurt like hell soon enough.

22

It's 2:07 a.m.

Can't quite believe I dozed off. Never thought I could, what with everything going on. Must be drained I guess, mind and body shutting down, recharging for the next horrific thing.

Josh is sleeping, half the wedding dress draped over his body, his head resting on Amelia's thigh. She's wide-awake, still sitting upright. Don't know how she's managed to stay like that without her back aching. Must be her age.

I sit up on the beam and stretch my arms up high, releasing the tension in my back and shoulders. "You okay, Amelia?" I ask, softly.

She just nods.

"How long has he been out?" I ask.

"A few hours"

"Good. Let's hope he sleeps a little longer. He needs it."

She nods. "Yeah."

I can tell she's struggling to cope, despite her brave, hardened expression. She's tough but not tough enough not to crack under such pressure. Not really sure how to deal with her. Should I leave her in silence? Or should I distract her with idle chitchat?

I don't do silence.

"So tell me about Michael and Juliet," I say. "What were they like?"

She shrugs. "They were all right."

"Better than the last family?"

"I *suppose*," she replies, a glint of suspicion in her eyes.

"How come?"

"Look, Cath, I know what you're trying to do but there's no need. I'm not a kid. I don't need you to take my mind off anything."

"But it's good. For both of us. We could use the distraction."

She shakes her head, scowling. "*No*, we don't. I'd rather have my mind *on* the situation. The last time I took my eye off the ball, my *dead* foster mum took a bite out of my brother."

"It wasn't your fault," I reassure her. "If anything, it was mine. I should have made sure that living-room was sealed off properly."

"With what?"

"I don't know. *Anything*. Or at least stayed downstairs, guarding it. Instead of lying on a bloody bed."

"None of this was your doing," Amelia says with conviction. "How could it be? You were the one who locked Juliet in the bedroom. You were the one who got the antiviral for Josh. And if it weren't for you then those Necs down there would have been up that ladder in a second. Josh was the one who left the bedroom door unlocked—*and I was the one who let the rotten bastards into the house.*"

"Look, if it weren't for you and your brother, I'd be another dead body, crawling around your garden. I owe you both my life. So whatever *mistakes* you think you've made tonight—I'm pretty sure we're all even. All right?"

Amelia falls silent.

"How about we go back to my distracting plan," I say with a slight smile. "You're really beginning to put a dampener on my evening. I was in a good mood before your started bumping your gums."

Amelia fights off a small grin, but I see it, buried beneath the dread, the horror, the claustrophobia of the attic. "You're crazy."

"And you're a lunatic," I say, lying back on the beam again, hands behind my head. "That's why we get along so bloody well."

I close my eyes, but I can tell she's still smiling.

* * *

The attic has been silent for the past few minutes, apart from the weak sound of footsteps and moans below.

I hear a squeak. Opening my eyes, I turn to see Amelia walking across the wood to the far corner of the roof, using the high beams for balance. "What are you doing?" I whisper. "Get back here. It's not safe to walk around."

"I'm looking for a way out of this attic."

"What are you talking about? The only way out is down through the hatch."

"Maybe we can break through the roof, and then crawl along the tiles."

"Are you mad? There's no way through. And even if there were, where the hell would we go? We'll be stuck on a bloody roof. We'd be worse off."

She starts to pull away some of the felt lining above her. "We could crawl along the roof, maybe climb down onto the neighbour's conservatory." She tugs hard, and a long strip comes away, dropping dust and debris all over her hair and shoulders. "And then we could drop into the garden and get the hell out of here."

I stand up on the beam, ready to stop her. "Amelia, come back over here. It's a stupid idea. You'll end up getting yourself killed."

"What's a stupid idea?" Josh asks as he sits up, his eyes half-shut, still not fully awake.

"Your sister thinks we should break through the roof and climb down the side of the house."

"It's not a stupid idea," she says. "The house is not that big, and next door's conservatory is not that far. We could do it."

"Amelia, please, come back over here," I plead. "You're making too much noise. They'll hear you."

"Who cares if they do? You said yourself that they can't get us up here."

"Yes, but as long as they know someone's up here, the longer they're likely to hang around."

"*Tough.* I'm doing this. My house. My rules."

"Can *I* help?" Josh asks, standing up on the wedding dress.

"Stay put, Josh," I say. "It's not—"

But before my words of warning leave my lips, I watch in horror as he steps on the weak flooring between the beams. His entire body rips through the floor and disappears out of sight.

"Oh, fucking hell!" I shout. "*Joooooosh!*"

Amelia races to the gaping hole, I quickly join her, staring at the bedroom, at least three metres down. With the kitchen knife still sticking out of her eye, Juliet looks up at us, her remaining eye drawn to the sound of my voice, and then to Josh as he lies on the floor, motionless, next to the double bed, pieces of ceiling plaster and broken wood on top of him.

Without a thought, I drop down into the hole, managing to land on the bed. As soon as my feet hit the mattress I feel my knee dislocate. I cry out in agony as I plunge off the bed, onto the carpet, just inches from Josh. In a split second Juliet is on me, blood and black tar oozing from her teeth. Grabbing her wrists, I try to push her off me. But she won't budge. All I can see is the horrid sight of her snapping jaws as they near me. And then I see Amelia, hanging from the hole in the ceiling, about to leap down to save her brother.

"No, Amelia!" I scream. "Stay up there! I need you to pull him up!" Every word that leaves my mouth brings Juliet closer.

And closer.

Amelia remains suspended for a moment, but then pulls herself back up into the attic.

Pressing my good knee into Juliet's stomach, I manage to lift her slightly off. And then, with every ounce of strength left, I thrust her body to the side. With both wrists still secure, and with the use of just one leg, I crawl to my feet. The pain in my knee is excruciating, but I still drive my boot into her throat, and hold it there, pulling as hard as I can on her arms. First I hear her neck snap, then both her shoulders pop out of their sockets. I keep pressing my foot into her throat until the skin around her neck begins to split.

I don't know what the plan is. I know I can't choke her. I know if her arms come off she's still the same threat. But I can't stop myself. I want to hurt her somehow. I don't care that she's already dead—she needs to suffer.

They all need to suffer.

Every last one of the rotten fuckers!

Blood starts to pool around my foot. But Juliet's eye is still very much open. "Why can't you just *die* you fucking bitch?"

The room is spinning. I think I'm going to pass out. Need to stop.

No. Not until she's nothing more than a stain!

Need to keep him safe.

The sound of deathly shrieks and heavy fists beating on the bedroom door pulls me out of my frenzy.

"Josh!" I hear Amelia scream. "Wake up! Please! You have to get up."

I see movement on the floor. It's Josh; he's

stirring. "Come on, Josh!" I hiss, knowing full well that my voice will bring about even more attention from the landing. "Wake up!"

He turns to me. There's a large gash on his forehead and blood is running down his face. His eyes open and straightaway he sees Juliet, her throat and jaw crushed beyond recognition. Screaming in terror, he scrambles away from her, his back against the bedside cabinet.

"Josh!" Amelia cries from above. "Get on the bed and I'll pull you up!"

Clearly disorientated, he takes in the events of the room—his restrained foster mother, the hole in the ceiling, and the bedroom door about to come off its hinges.

"Move, Josh!" I yell. "They're coming! Get on the fucking bed!"

Too terrified even to cry, he leaps onto the mattress and reaches up to his sister's arm. But it's too far, his fingers are about a foot away.

"Jump!" she yells. "Come on!"

Fragments of broken wood fly off the doorframe. The lock is seconds from shattering.

Josh jumps, but merely brushes his fingers along her open palm. He starts to panic, tears of frustration—of horror as more wood sprays onto the carpet.

I let go of Juliet's arms, and I pull my boot away from the mush where her neck used to be. But she's still very much alive, snapping her broken jaw with what remains of her teeth. *Need to hold the door shut.* I try to move but she grabs my boot with both hands. My legs give way. I cry out in pain, but I still keep crawling, using the bed to steer me.

"Come on, Josh!" Amelia shouts. "You're nearly there!"

Each leap brings him closer and closer to his sister's grasp.

I can't shake my leg from Juliet's vice-like hold, so I drag my body along the carpet towards the door, towing her behind me.

"*I can't do it!*" Josh cries, failing yet another attempt. "*It's too high!*"

I reach back and start to pry Juliet's fingers from me, but her nails have clamped on too tight.

"*They're almost in!*" Josh bellows as several Nec

arms worm their way through the small gap between the door and the frame. *"They're gonna get me!"*

"No they're not, bro!" his sister shouts. "Forget about them! They're just dumb cows in a field! Remember! They're nothing! Focus on me!"

"I can't do it!"

"Yes, you can! You're my brother! And you can do *anything!* Foster kids never give up! And we're not scared of *no one!"*

He tries again, managing to grab a finger, but he slips back down immediately.

I quickly untie the lace of my boot and wrench my foot out, freeing me from Juliet's clutches.

The lock flies off and the door bursts open.

"Oh, shit!" Amelia cries. "They're in!"

A stampede of Necs storms the bedroom, fighting to squeeze through the doorway. I crawl onto the bed, moments before they reach it. Somehow I stand, taking Josh by the waist and picking his tiny body up just as a Nec bites into my exposed foot. I don't feel the pain as its teeth rip through my sock, sinking into my flesh, or the despair as another rotter bites into my neck, spraying blood over the quilt. All I feel is a sense of relief as I watch Amelia pull her brother up into the attic, safe, away from the monsters.

Away from me.

Unable to stand any longer, I fall backwards with the heft of Necs all around me. The back of my head slams onto the floor, but I stay fixated on the horde of creatures, scrambling to take another chunk out of me. But I won't let them eat. They can infect me; they can even have a taste. But that's all. I'm nobody's food.

If you want this free dinner, you're gonna have to work for it!

Using the bed, I pull myself back onto my feet. I push my thumbs into the eye sockets of the first Nec, blinding it. Throwing a hard punch, I demolish the jaw of another. And another. I can no longer hear their roars, their cries of hunger. As I limp and fight through the dead, I catch the odd glimpse of Amelia staring down in horror from the ceiling, screaming something inaudible, with her sobbing brother at her side. I'm out of the bedroom, onto the landing. I have nothing left to throw at them.

My arms are numb; my knee has stopped functioning. I don't feel anything when I collapse, headfirst down the stairs, taking several Necs with me.

At the bottom, all I can focus on is the attic hatch. *Please let them be okay.*

Amelia, never leave your brother's side. And never change. You don't deserve any of this.

Josh, stay innocent. Don't let this nightmare change you.

I wish I had time to say goodbye, but I don't.

There's no time for anything. I've done everything I can. Help will come for them.

But not for me.

My shift is over.

EPILOGUE

I know I'm limping severely, but the pain in my knee has vanished. I don't remember how I made it outside, but I did. I look down at my foot—it's bleeding heavily. I pat the side of my neck. More blood. But again—I don't feel any pain...

* * *

As I drag my leg along the pavement, past the parked cars, I see Necs walking beside me. Women, children, men, almost a perfect blend of humanity, lost to this horrifying disease in the space of a day. Each one has no interest in my flesh...

* * *

I can no longer remember where I've been. I still know my name. It's Catherine. Catherine Woods. And I remember the faces of my friends, my family. But that's it. I have no idea where I am or what the hell I'm doing here...

* * *

The stench of decay is all around me, getting thicker, as if my sense of smell is getting stronger. The pack of Necs that walk beside is growing with every blackout, with every…

* * *

I see lights up ahead. And people. A wall of people. With guns. The Necs start to sprint towards them. I follow, but without the speed. Shot after shot hits the dead, dropping them to the concrete. Some of them have made it to the people, sinking their teeth into their exposed skin. There's blood.

Lots of blood…

* * *

I'm alone. I've wandered into a strange garden. Don't know what happened to the other Necs. Most of them scattered. My thoughts are slipping away by the second. But I still know my name. It's Catherine. Catherine Woods….

* * *

I'm standing by a large window, trying to see inside a house. Suddenly a little girl looks back at me through the glass. She has long black hair to her shoulders. She's afraid of me…

* * *

I see a man. Her father perhaps? He's afraid of me. I no longer see the darkness of the garden. All I see is red. *I'm hungry*. I chase the man to the back door of the house…

* * *

The little girl—she's terrified. She's holding something. A weapon. It looks like a golf putt. I don't feel the pain as she drives it into my face, splitting my nose open. All I see is *flesh*. I try to bite down on the man's arm but he fights back. I'm so close.

So hungry…

* * *

Something sharp pierces the back of my skull. A bullet? I don't feel the pain. I barely feel anything. The red has vanished. The night has returned. But not for long. As I crash onto the ground, I stare up at the stars...

* * *

I hear the voice of the little girl. "*I know what I want to be when I grow up,*" she tells her father...

* * *

My eyes shut and the darkness comes. But I still know my name. It's...

Coming Soon

From Steven Jenkins

BURN THE DEAD: RIOT

To receive emails on all future book releases, please
subscribe to: www.steven-jenkins.com

About the Author

Steven Jenkins was born in the small Welsh town of Llanelli, where he began writing stories at the age of eight, inspired by '80s horror movies and novels by *Richard Matheson*.

During Steven's teenage years, he became a great lover of writing dark and twisted poems—six of which gained him publications with *Poetry Now*, *Brownstone Books*, and *Strong Words*.

Over the next few years, as well as becoming a husband and father, Steven spent his free time writing short stories, achieving further publication with *Dark Moon Digest*. His terrifying tales of the afterlife and zombies gained him positive reviews, particularly his story, *Burning Ambition*, which also came runner up in a *Five-Stop-Story* contest. And in 2014 his debut novel, *Fourteen Days* was published by Barking Rain Press.

You can find out more about Steven Jenkins at his website: www.steven-jenkins.com or on Facebook: www.facebook.com/stevenjenkinsauthor and on Twitter: twitter.com/Author_Jenkins

OTHER TITLES
BY STEVEN JENKINS

FOURTEEN DAYS

Workaholic developer Richard Gardener is laid up at home for two week's mandatory leave—doctor's orders. No stress. No computers. Just fourteen days of complete rest.

Bliss for most, but hell for Richard… in more ways than one. There's a darkness that lives inside Richard's home; a presence he never knew existed because he was seldom there alone.

Did he just imagine those footsteps? The smoke alarm shrieking?

The woman in his kitchen?

His wife thinks that he's just suffering from

work withdrawal, but as the days crawl by in his solitary confinement, the terror seeping through the walls continues to escalate—threatening his health, his sanity, and his marriage.

When the inconceivable no longer seems quite so impossible, Richard struggles to come to terms with what is happening and find a way to banish the darkness—before he becomes an exile in his own home.

"Gripping, tense, and bloody scary. The author has taken the classic ghost story, and blended it faultlessly with Hitchcock's Rear Window."

COLIN DAVIES
DIRECTOR OF BBC'S BAFTA
WINNING: THE COALHOUSE

"Fourteen Days is the most purely enjoyable novel I've read in a very long time."

RICHARD BLANDFORD
THE WRITER'S WORKSHOP &
AUTHOR OF HOUND DOG

Available at:
www.steven-jenkins.com,
Amazon UK, Amazon US,
and all other book retailers.

Robert Stephenson makes his living burning zombies—a job that pays the bills and plays tricks on the mind. Still, his life is routine until one day his infected wife, Anna, shows up in line for the incinerator, and Rob must cremate the love of his life.

In a race against the clock, he must find his four-year-old son Sammy, who is stranded in a newly quarantined zone, teeming with the walking dead, and crawling with the Necro-Morbus virus.

Does Rob have what it takes to fight the undead and put his broken family back together?

Or will he also end up in the incinerator—

burning with the rest of the dead?

"If you're looking for a fast-paced zombie read, I highly recommend Burn the Dead by Steven Jenkins (5-STARS)"

K.C. FINN

READERS' FAVORITE

Available at:

www.steven-jenkins.com

Amazon UK, Amazon US

and all other book retailers.

SPINE

Listen closely. A creak, almost too light to be heard...was it the shifting of an old house, or footsteps down the hallway? Breathe softly, and strain to hear through the silence. That breeze against your neck might be a draught, or an open window.

Slip into the pages of SPINE and you'll be persuaded to leave the lights on and door firmly bolted. From Steven Jenkins, bestselling author of *Fourteen Days* and *Burn the Dead*, this horror collection of eight stories go beyond the realm of terror to an entirely different kind of creepiness. Beneath innocent appearances lurk twisted minds and scary monsters, from soft scratches behind the wall, to the paranoia of walking through a crowd and knowing that every single eye is locked on you. In this world, voices lure lost souls to the cliff's edge and illicit drugs offer glimpses of things few should see. Scientists tamper with the afterlife, and the strange happenings at a nursing home are not what they first seem.

So don't let that groan from the closet fool you—the monster is hiding right where you least expect it.

"If you love scary campfire stories of ghosts, demonology, and all things that go bump in the night, then you'll love this horror collection by author Steven Jenkins."

COLIN DAVIES
DIRECTOR OF BBC'S BAFTA
WINNING: THE COALHOUSE

Available at:
www.steven-jenkins.com,
Amazon UK, Amazon US,
and all other book retailers.

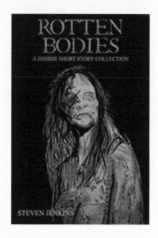

We all fear death's dark spectre, but in a zombie apocalypse, dying is a privilege reserved for the lucky few. There are worse things than a bullet to the brain—*much* worse.

The dead are walking, and they're hungry. Steven Jenkins, bestselling author of *Fourteen Days* and *Burn The Dead*, shares six zombie tales that are rotten for all the right reasons.

Meet Dave, a husband and father with a dirty secret, who quickly discovers that lies aren't only dangerous…they're deadly. Athlete Sarah once ran for glory, but when she finds herself alone on a country road with an injured knee, second place is as good as last. Working in a cremation facility, Rob likes to peek secretly at the faces of his inventory before they're turned to ash. When it comes to workplace health and sanity, however, some rules are better left unbroken. Howard, shovelling coal in the darkness of a Welsh coal mine, knows something's amiss when his colleagues begin to disappear. But it's when the lights come on that things get truly scary.

Six different takes on the undead, from the grotesque to the downright terrifying. But reader beware: as the groans get louder and the twitching starts, you'll be *dying* to reach the final page.

"Utterly hair-raising, in all its gory glory!"

CATE HOGAN

AUTHOR OF ONE SUMMER

Available at:
www.steven-jenkins.com,
Amazon UK, Amazon US,
and all other book retailers.

Printed in Great Britain
by Amazon.co.uk, Ltd.,
Marston Gate.